Praise for *Man with a Seagull on His Head*

"All the lonely people, where do they all come from? This lovely, evocative, slim novel about the way humans connect to each other is heart-rendingly beautiful. Every sentence in this book is perfect."—**Mary Cotton, Newtonville Books (Newton, MA)**

"Reading Harriet Paige in advance feels like I've been privy to a special secret. I'm so glad I finally get to share this book with the world."—**Lesley Rains, City of Asylum Bookstore (Pittsburgh, PA)**

"A quirky, interesting, original story of life lived one foot in front of the other."—**Beth Carpenter, The Country Bookshop (Southern Pines, NC)**

"Truly unique. A quirky and intelligent read with a deep beating heart."—**Kevin Elliott, Seminary Co-op Bookstore (Chicago, IL)**

"It's a rare novel that reminds you of one by Virginia Woolf and doesn't fall short in the comparison. Makes ordinary life seem perpetually on the edge of epiphany."—**Laurie Greer, Politics & Prose Bookstore (Washington, DC)**

"The story sings off the page with tender lyricism. This is a quirky gem."—**Linda McLoughlin Figel, {pages} a bookstore (Manhattan Beach, CA)**

"The opening of *Man with a Seagull on His Head* tempts you with its brisk prose and summery seaside setting to pick it up as a momentary diversion, but it quickly establishes powerful links among its many characters, connecting hearts and minds across distance, time, and cultural barriers."—**James Crossley, Island Books (Mercer Island, WA)**

"A beautiful fable about art and inspiration and humanity. Outsider artist Ray Eccles has something of Melville's Bartleby about him, but the narrative—smartly—focuses on those whose lives he influences. A gorgeously written, tender debut novel."—**Lexi Beach, Astoria Bookshop (Astoria, NY)**

"Anyone interested in the mysteries of memory, art-making, and missed connections will be charmed by Harriet Paige's odd, funny, and wise parable."—**John Francisconi, Bank Square Books (Mystic, CT)**

"Explores the somewhat psychotic lengths inspiration can take someone paired with the exploitative facets of the art world—and it's rendered with such a fantastic combination of distance and intimacy. The world could maybe be made better if more seagulls fell on our heads."—**Rebecca George, Volumes Bookcafe (Chicago, IL)**

"You want to extend a hand and wish the characters well. A fine read. Refreshingly recommend."—**Todd Miller, Arcadia Books (Spring Green, WI)**

"*Man with a Seagull on His Head* is an enthralling read unlike anything I have ever read. It makes you feel crazy, sane, upset, and euphoric. Harriet Paige is a remarkable writer with an amazing muse."—**Nick Buzanski, Book Culture (New York, NY)**

"Sad, hopeful, perfectly poignant and because the internal mechanics of the novel are so well metred, it also ends beautifully. With echoes of Brian Moore's Judith Hearne and a bit of Marilynne Robinson's Lila, Harriet Paige is more than a writer to watch. She has arrived."—**David Worsley, Words Worth Books (Waterloo, ON)**

"The compelling characters, fable-like pacing, and funny take on "outsider" art keep the pages flying by."—**Pete Mulvihill, Green Apple Books (San Francisco, CA)**

"Lovely, quiet, and quite beautiful. I found myself slowly reading so that I wouldn't miss any poetic descriptions of people and places. Admittedly, it's a hard novel to pin down—is it a mystery? A family story? A story of mental illness and art? It's unlike anything I've read, really, and I find it hard to describe and truly convey its beauty."—**Sarah Letke, Redbery Books (Cable, WI)**

"If you like your fiction smart and surreal, you will love *Man with a Seagull on His Head*. A strong, compelling debut!"—**Carol Schneck Varner, Schuler Books and Music (Okemos, MI)**

"So many wonderful things in one book! It is an odd, well-written, fully realized, moving and unsettling novel. It reminded me of Tom McCarthy's novel *Remainder*. A rather brilliant first novel; I will be watching for Harriet Paige's next offering."—**Susan Chamberlain, The Book Keeper (Sarnia, ON)**

"A deeply thoughtful quick read. Harriet Paige has crafted a diverse array of characters, each captivating as they bare their most vulnerable moments and stand firmly in moments of surety or pride. This rich novel kept me company long after I put it down."—**Carrie Koepke, Skylark Bookshop (Columbia, MO)**

MAN WITH A SEAGULL ON HIS HEAD

MAN WITH A SEAGULL ON HIS HEAD

By Harriet Paige

BIBLIOASIS
WINDSOR, ON

Library and Archives Canada Cataloguing in Publication

Paige, Harriet, author
        Man with a seagull on his head / Harriet Paige.

Originally published: Hebden Bridge, Bluemoose Books Ltd., 2017.
Issued in print and electronic formats.
ISBN 978-1-77196-239-1 (softcover)
ISBN 978-1-77196-240-7 (ebook)

        I. Title.

PR6116.A44M36 2018   823'.92   C2018-901719-8
                                             C2018-901720-1

Readied for the press by Daniel Wells
Copy-edited by Jessica Faulds
Cover designed by Zoe Norvell
Typeset by Chris Andrechek

PRINTED AND BOUND IN CANADA

For Joseph, Anton, Tabitha, and Cosmo

One

For a short time you couldn't go to the opening night of an art exhibition without someone mentioning Ray Eccles. It didn't matter if it was at The Tate gallery or some loft in Clerkenwell, someone had something to say about the Eccles portraits. Which is impressive if you remember how conventional they really are. No shock tactics needed. Of course the materials he used weren't conventional. And maybe you remember how many young artists around that time—which was the early 1980s, before the Young British Artists broke onto the scene—tried to copy him in that respect. For a while it seemed every art-college student in the country was using the contents of their kitchen cupboards to paint with, in the hope that they'd capture some of Eccles' raw power.

In June 1976, though, there was nothing interesting about Ray Eccles. It's true; he knew it himself as well as anyone. The interesting thing was just about to happen.

It wouldn't have happened at all if it hadn't been for the Water Board, which had moved into Belvedere Close to do something to the pipes, something that involved shutting off the water all day, which was quite inconvenient since it was a Saturday.

That day, which was the 12th of June, was also his birthday although that didn't interest him much, even though it was the big four-zero. All that meant was that he was now past the age when anything interesting was likely to happen to him, and by interesting he meant the kind of thing other people might consider pretty normal, pretty uninteresting really. Like getting married. Having a child perhaps, although probably not. Ray was an only child. His parents, too, had both been only children and, having found himself solitary at the tip of such a neat, straight branch of the family tree, it seemed like it had fallen to him to put a stop to things rather than spill over into new generations. There wasn't a lot of point in prolonging things, in his opinion. Getting something done, out the way, finished with: this was what got him through his days, whether that something be the washing up or burying his mother or, if he had thought much about it, his own presence in the world.

He'd been a late arrival in an unhappy marriage, an embarrassing and binding reminder of a final, desperate grasp at intimacy on his father's part. The union continued as an extended standoff. Mr. and Mrs. Eccles dominated their son with silence. And although he found some solace in corners and small places, he grew up, effectively, in a waiting room—life, he understood, was something to be got through, and his mother had finally got through hers only a month ago, when Ray had at last left the family home and moved into Belvedere Close.

His house was number eight, although it wasn't a house but a bungalow like all the others in the Close, and it wasn't his, either, but his Auntie Mary's—not a real auntie (he didn't have any of those) but a friend of his mother's, although not much of a friend either, for Mrs. Eccles had never had a good word to say about her. She could never understand why Auntie Mary had to go and live in Shoeburyness for a start. Why not choose Prittlewell, as she had done, or, better still, Rochford, both of them tucked tidily inland rather than lolling out of the mouth of the Thames towards the open sea—all that salt and wind couldn't be good for anyone.

Auntie Mary no longer had the salt and wind to contend with though, because she had moved up to Cumbria to be near her niece, Claire. Unlike Mrs. Eccles, who, without ever having expressed any pleasure at being in her son's company, had seen to it that he never left home, Auntie Mary had waved her own daughter, Louise, off to a better life in Australia, leaving her to Claire and the care home in Cumbria. She kept hold of the bungalow in Belvedere Close because, she told Ray, she might want to come back one day, but until she did (until she died, he understood) she was happy for him to live in it for a minimal rent.

There were many things in Auntie Mary's house. China ladies with geese at their feet, bunny rabbits sitting on leaves, little mice nibbling cheese. Ray tried his best to keep out of their way, although it didn't occur to him to move them or anything else, not even Auntie Mary's many, many photographs, which he could have done without having to look at every day: Louise as a baby, Louise as a little girl, as a teenager at school, with the Australian, and now the baby. Louise and Ray used to play together as children and Auntie Mary would joke that they'd marry one day—until it became clear just how much of a joke it really was. When he'd first arrived, he'd stood for a while and smelled the air in the room with the double bed that he imagined Louise sharing with the Australian on her visits. But thereafter he'd kept that door shut.

Today he woke early, at six-thirty, in order to be out of the house by the time the water went off at eight. The lack of water was impetus for an excursion he'd been contemplating for a while: a trip to East Beach, to the open sea. He'd had it in mind that East Beach was somewhere he'd like to go ever since he'd overheard them talking at work about an unexploded bomb that was lying there under the water. Just a rumour, they'd said, but why else was there a line of posts running out from the shore into the sea at the far end of the beach? It was to stop swimmers or boats from entering the danger area, they said. It would be the end of Shoeburyness if that went off, they said. And the girl whose name was Frances said it was enough to put you off living there. "Don't you live in Shoebury, Ray?"

There were few places that Ray felt comfortable, and standing at his Xerox machine when they got to chatting and carrying on around him like this was certainly not one of them. But standing by the edge of the sea knowing that there was an unexploded bomb sitting there underneath was somewhere he'd like to be. He thought that bomb might be good company.

Plenty of curtains were still shut tight in the Close when he left the house, and he wondered if others had forgotten about the water going off. The possibility gave him a small puff of pleasure; he thought of Mrs. Foyle rising to find there was nothing to fill the kettle and realising it was too late for a bath. He didn't dislike his neighbours but did his best to avoid them, all the same. They'd come, each of them, bearing casseroles and condolences and to make themselves known: Mrs. Foyle, Mrs. Hinton, Mrs. Coates, Mrs. Timms, Mrs. Robinson. Most of these Mrs. had a Mr., and they were all of an age not to work anymore, which made it a rare occasion that he could leave the bungalow and not have to smile or raise his hand or make a remark about the weather. Being out early with not a single one of them pottering around their front gardens pouring bath water on the flowerbeds or bringing the milk in from the step was as good a start to the day as he could have hoped for, and it even made him believe there might be a bit of breeze in the air, a tiny tremor that could grow and mount an uprising against this dreadful heat.

He left the Close and turned onto Elm Road. So far it was familiar territory, but the awareness that he'd have to branch out at some stage was already tingeing his surroundings with a trace of the unknown. His life here had worked out a certain route, like the number nine bus, from which there had not yet been reason to deviate. He went from number eight Belvedere Close to the bus stop on Elm Road, where he caught the bus to the Civic Centre in Southend where he worked, and occasionally walked on a little further to the High Street and the little row of shops there that saw him through the week. That was it. He knew the sea was somewhere beyond, he could even smell it sometimes, but he had never been there.

He passed his bus stop and the sight of it, empty, made him wonder if he had a job anymore. Mr. Turner had not really made that clear yesterday. "Give yourself some time" had been his precise words. Some time. Ray said the words again to himself, and whereas yesterday they'd sounded like something that could be counted in days or weeks, they sounded today like a long time—indefinite, infinite, for how would he know when some time was over?

His job was to serve the photocopying requirements of Southend District Council, who were based now in the new Civic Centre off Victoria Parade in Southend. He considered himself good at this job and did not like to think others thought differently, especially when their reasons for doing so were unjustified.

The office he worked in was on the ground floor of the Civic Centre, just a few doors down the corridor from the main reception. He shared the room with four other people. He knew the names of these people, which were Pamela, Frances, Paula and Mr. Turner, and he knew that Mr. Turner was in charge, but, beyond typing and talking on the telephone, he didn't know what any of them did. This didn't worry him, nor did the fact that their desks were all a lot bigger than his and grouped congenially beneath the room's two large but permanently blinded windows. He was on the opposite wall alongside the door, separated from his colleagues by a large area of rough brown carpet, marked here and there by darker patches representing accidents with the tea and coffee tray. His own desk could hardly be called a desk at all, it being just a small square table by the side of the Xerox machine, identical to the tea and coffee table on the other side. It was never referred to as "Ray's desk" by his colleagues, but always "the Xerox table." He did, however, have a chair to sit on while he waited for a big run to go through, and this chair, which was made of brown plastic with a brown cushioned seat, was of exactly the same sort as those sat on by everyone else in the office, including Mr. Turner.

That the tea and coffee table resided in his area pointed, in Paula's mind, to the fact that he should be the one to make the tea and coffee. In her opinion, it was a duty she should have relinquished to him along with the photocopying when she was promoted from his position to one of the desks under the window. All this he knew from her mutterings and sighs and "accidents" with the milk all over his photocopying pile, although he had never been asked to make a cup of tea and had never refused to make one. It had not been listed as one of his duties and, since he made a point of not drinking tea in the office himself, he saw no reason why he should make it for others.

As far as he was concerned there were only two sides to his job. One was to keep the forms topped up, and each morning he checked the grey plastic trays arranged along one wall of the office to see if they were running low. Any fewer than five and he'd take one out and make a further fifty copies to ensure they never ran out. The other side was to fulfil the Xerox orders given to him by council workers throughout the entire building. These arrived in his tray, located on a small table in the corridor just outside the door. Whatever it was that needed Xeroxing would be accompanied by a small white slip giving space for people to write how many copies were required, their initials, the department to which it should be returned, and whether or not the sheets should be stapled.

It was not an easy job keeping track of all these bits of paper, and in the springtime especially, when demand for forms was at its highest, it could take most of the morning just keeping the trays topped up, which meant a buildup of orders for the afternoon. And everyone thought their order should have priority. Even though the Xerox slips had a clear format, it was not unusual for people to depart from it in an attempt to grab his attention, using red pen for instance, or underlining the number of copies with a couple of strong black lines, or putting a scribbled star next to it, or going so far as to write "urgent" across the top. He had even, while walking down the corridor back from the Gents, caught people interfering with the queuing system, putting their document to the bottom of the pile as if it had been there all morning. He never said anything on these occasions, just slipped the papers back into the correct order once they'd gone, knowing that only under direct instruction from Mr. Turner could a document jump the Xerox queue.

Yesterday, all had gone as usual at first. There were already orders in his tray when he arrived in the morning but he dealt with the forms first, as always. He checked in every tray, he was certain, doing fifty copies of those that were running low. So he was most confused when Paula, who was over by the trays just before lunchtime, turned round and said, "Ray, we've run out of PA147s."

This had not happened before. It was his job to prevent this from happening.

"We've run out of PA147s," she said again, although this time she looked past Ray to Mr. Turner.

"What's happened, Ray?" asked Mr. Turner, looking up from his coffee.

"We've run out of PA147s," Ray repeated.

"Yes, so I hear. *Why* have we run out of PA147s?"

"I don't know, I only just finished topping them all up."

"Not quite all, it seems. It's your job to prevent this from happening. It's hardly a difficult job, now is it? You'd better go down to reception and hope there's a master."

Reception was where the master copies of all the council's forms were kept although, as Paula had told him in a final whispered warning, "they don't have copies of *everything*." A trip to reception to try your luck on the lottery of their filing system was something to be avoided at all costs; that was what all the counting and checking and being on the safe side was for.

He could feel the pin pricks of sweat gathering in his palm as he left the office and started down the corridor. The receptionist smiled at him as he approached. She was a young girl with a lot of hair and pale shimmering lips, who said "Good morning!" at him each day in a bright, insistent way. He preferred to be ignored and usually was; this relentless greeting seemed to him to have menacing intent.

"We don't have copies of everything, you know," she said, in a voice that made his ear lobes hot. He focused his attention on the board of headshots mounted on the wall next to the counter and found Mr. Turner in his younger days. His slightly tilted head and questioning gaze seemed to have his words attached to it, *it's hardly a difficult job now is it*, so he looked away at the girl, now riffling among the forms, having to stand on tiptoes to see inside the drawer of the filing cabinet.

"PA147 you say."

"Yes," he said, and she sent the drawer rolling back in. He wished he could try another number.

"Well then, you're in luck," she said, spinning round on her heel with the form held aloft. She lowered it towards the counter, then whipped it away again above her head. "What's it worth?"

This was worse. She was waiting for him to say something witty. He thought of making a quick manoeuvre around the end of the counter and grabbing the form from her, then decided it would be easier to jump up and snatch it from where he was. But just as he was gearing up for it she said, "Ah, look at you," and laid it gently on the counter in front of him, taking her hands clear away and behind her back.

"Don't forget to bring it back," she called after him as he started on his return journey up the corridor. "That's when the trouble starts, when people don't bring back the masters."

It was true: it was not a good day for him. He never really got back on track after the business with the PA147s. He got orders confused, did too few of one, too many of another, forgot to staple, returned them to the wrong people. And when things started going wrong like that, well, you were always on the catch up, the new orders piling up while you put right your mistakes.

At the end of the day, Mr. Turner asked if he could have a word. As the others filed past on their way out they said, "Goodbye, Ray," and, "See you on Monday, Ray," and there was something consoling in the addition of his name that made him suspect something already. Mr. .Turner stretched out his arm to indicate the empty chair on the other side of his desk and Ray went over, avoiding the gaze that took him back to junior school, the teacher looking at him quizzically as if searching for an explanation for his existence.

"I've noticed things haven't really been going your way today, Ray," said Mr. Turner when they were both seated.

"I checked the trays this morning. I think someone must have removed all the PA147s. I think they did it on purpose."

"Now, Ray, don't let's get childish. These are the offices of Southend District Council, not a junior school. Why on earth would someone do that?"

"I don't know, Mr. Turner."

"Quite." Mr. Turner interlaced his fingers and placed his hands on the desk. "Anyway, it wasn't just the forms, was it? It was the orders as well. You couldn't keep on top of them."

Ray noticed Mr. Turner had dirt under his fingernails.

"Frances said she saw you crying today."

And also those little white flecks that showed you didn't drink enough milk.

"I know about your mother, Ray. I don't know why you didn't tell me."

He could feel something edging down his nostril. He'd have to sniff in a moment to stop it emerging. He screwed up his nose to try and slow its passage, and tilted his head a little upwards.

"I think maybe you should stay home for a bit. Give yourself some time."

"Yes," said Ray, careful not to lower his chin.

He wanted Mr. Turner to go now so he could blow his nose. He heard his chair push back promisingly against the rough carpet but then watched with dismay as Mr. Turner walked round the end of the desk towards him. He put a hand on Ray's back. "We really value what you do here, Ray," he said, and gave him a little pat. "We're all thinking of you."

Ray sat at his Xerox table when Mr. Turner had finally gone. He had a bit of tidying up to do. There were papers muddled all over the place and they needed to be sorted into piles, their slips attached ready to be returned to the relevant departments on Monday morning. When he'd finished he stayed sitting there in the empty office, listening to the vacuum cleaner making its way down the corridor outside. He looked around the room, and the personal clutter of other people's desks did a good job, in his colleagues' absence, of making him feel he was not alone. If he felt like sobbing or lying down flat on his back on the bare brown carpet in the middle of the room, then the pen pots and photographs, the potted plants, dirty mugs and pulled-out chairs kept him sitting quietly right where he was.

He'd left the High Street behind him and was carrying on in the general direction of the sea. Off his regular tracks now, he started to take notice of things: a woman putting a bucket of fishing nets outside a newsagent; a man in shorts walking a dog; a red car passing noisily; the Shoeburyness Hotel, closed; the smell of the sea, quite pungent, in the air; a faded blue sign reading "East Beach" and pointing down a narrow dusty path with long yellow grass growing up on either side. He made his way down the path, observing his feet and the dust that drifted up over his shoes as he walked. Then he looked up and saw the sea.

He had arrived. And as he walked onward across the open patch of empty grassland before him he was struck by a sense of uncertainty, of not knowing how to behave or what he was doing here. For a moment he stood quite still. He looked at his watch. It was nearly eight. Seven thirty in the evening, when the water would go back on, was a long way off. He looked up and saw a sort of shack, which was at least something to aim for, so he walked towards it. He found a board displaying ice creams nailed up on one side and a bicycle propped against another. From here he could see the actual beach at last: the bank fell away to a narrow band of greyish shingle, dirtied by dried seaweed and plastic bottles but nicer than the beaches he passed on the bus to work each morning, which turned to mud flats when the tide was out. There was no road here: it finished a little way behind him and was replaced by a track leading to a dusty patch that looked like it would do for parking. Other than that, the beach was backed only by the large area of parched, unkempt grass he'd just crossed. Now that he'd been here for a few minutes he was starting to find it quite pleasant.

In the distance, at the far end of the beach, he could see the posts running out into the sea just as his colleagues had described. He set off towards them, choosing to stick to the grass rather than descend onto the shingle. The girl in his office, Frances, entered his mind. She had a lot of freckles— like grains of sand, he thought. There was definitely a bit of breeze here, pushing in from the sea. He could feel it against his right cheek. He could feel the sun there too, and was mildly aware of the skin on that side of his face responding.

It didn't take him long to reach the posts, which continued all the way up onto the grass, blocking off the final fifty yards or so of the beach before a rough and stony bank rose sharply to mark the end. It wouldn't have taken much to get across onto the other side of the barrier but he was satisfied with being here, on this side, where he could still look clearly upon the prohibited section of the sea and picture the bomb lying beneath like a bloated fish. He sat down on the grass but, uncomfortable and not sure what to do with his legs, he switched to kneeling and remained there, upright and staring straight out to sea. It calmed him to think that the sea held a secret. If he had been the sort to examine things further, he might have seen that it had to do with the latent promise of death, of being able to feel it advancing within him upon another plane of existence, perhaps now ready to reveal itself, like an old friend whose warmth was remembered but whose face had been forgotten. But he felt these things in his blood, not in his brain, and merely found himself, for once, watchful and at ease.

He gazed farther out towards the misty horizon and up at the sky, blank and thick with the heat. And then down again across the wide, ruffled water, the sunlight caught upon its irregular peaks. The sea never stops, he thought. This thought might have led to other thoughts, for he was beginning to get used to them, had not a woman suddenly stood up in his view. That another human being should just appear like this on the beach in front, so close when there was the whole empty stretch available, alarmed and bewildered him into believing her for a moment to be some strange creature of the sea. The word mermaid darted into his head like a minnow—and then just as quickly out again, for anyone could see she was no such thing. Still, he felt her significance, obscurely but keenly. That she had somehow been placed there. Placed there for him. She stood with her back to him looking out towards the water, her arms hanging down but slightly removed from her sides in a rather unnatural way. The grass bank cut off her legs from view, but her top half was clothed in a white blouse, blown to one side by the wind which, clearly stronger down there, caught also on her sandy hair and lifted it clear of her neck.

He waited, still kneeling on the grass.

Then she turned her head and looked straight at him, and at that moment he felt a sharp jab on his head because a seagull had fallen from the sky and changed everything.

Two

Amanda Parsons had been working as a junior reporter for the *Southend Evening Echo* for a whole month before she came across a lead for a possible story, something that might free her from the inglorious task of compiling the information box—a small panel at the bottom of the letters page giving tide times, weather forecast, and telephone numbers for the Samaritans and Marriage Guidance—which was all she'd been put in charge of for now.

Of all people, it was her best friend Ruth who gave her the opportunity she'd been waiting for. They were sitting with lemon ices on a bench outside Keddies department store where, before Amanda had got the job at the *Echo*, the two of them had worked together in household linens. Ruth was still there, although no longer in household linens. She'd been transferred up to haberdashery and that morning her new boss, Jennifer Mulholland, had told her something: she'd seen a bird fall out of the sky and land on a man's head.

"It's not funny actually," said Ruth in that earnest way of hers when Amanda laughed. "The man was quite badly injured."

But it was funny. The injury made it all the funnier, and definitely more newsworthy. Immediately Amanda recalled her editor, Larry, unleashing his wheezy laugh into the office upon being told the story of the group of girls whose topless frolic in Southchurch Park pond had been interrupted when they were attacked by a swan. "Love it!" he'd said, slapping his hand down on the desk. This story was not all that dissimilar. It was bizarre. It involved a bird. No topless girls unfortunately… but maybe she could stretch the truth. Maybe if Jennifer Mulholland had been sunbathing. Topless? And then she laughed again, for that really was funny.

Jennifer Mulholland had worked at Keddies forever. Ruth and Amanda thought her a curious creature. Each morning they watched as she crossed household linens on the ground floor and slowly mounted the stairs to the haberdashery department on the third, her backside tightly and impenetrably packaged in stuffy homemade skirt suits that took no account of the stiflingly hot weather. In the dead hours between three and five in the afternoon they sometimes fell to amusing themselves with simple conjecture about her private moments. For some reason they found it hilarious just to imagine Miss Mulholland getting drunk, or having sex, or even just being naked. When Ruth was transferred to haberdashery, Amanda ordered her friend to do some digging but all Ruth could unearth was that Miss Mulholland had once been the Southend Carnival Queen.

Amanda had choked on her cigarette. "No way!"

"Miss Southend 1955."

"You've got to be joking."

"No! She's even promised to bring in a newspaper clipping. She was eighteen years old, which makes her—"

"Thirty-nine. Nearly forty!"

Back in Ruth's bedsit that afternoon, where they wasted much of their time, the two girls imagined Miss Southend

1955 in a string of lustful encounters: behind carnival floats, beneath bandstands, below the pier. But these scenarios, developed in the slow hilarious haze of dope, didn't stand up next to the reality of Jennifer herself, and they came to the conclusion that her window of romantic opportunity had more likely been filled with demurely fought-off fumbles, all in the name of saving herself for a husband who never came. Jennifer Mulholland was surely still a virgin. Amanda could tell. When you'd done it you could immediately spot someone who hadn't.

"Of course I shall have to interview her," said Amanda when she and Ruth had finished discussing the story's merits and her proposed breakthrough onto the news pages. Ruth said she would come too, for she had nothing else to do that afternoon.

Amanda had imagined Jennifer in a bungalow, but the reality was a bedsit not much bigger that Ruth's and not far from it either, in one of those big dingy old houses set back from the seafront in the part of Southend known as Westcliff-on-Sea. As in Ruth's building, the hallways and stairs were in a state of communal neglect. The brown gloss paint on the bannisters was heavily chipped as if wilfully and idly picked at, and the walls had gathered mysterious stains which made the embossed wallpaper look as if it had swelled with an accumulation of smoke and sweat and boozy breath. Amanda knew that people lived in such places. Ruth lived in such a place. But that Jennifer Mulholland should do so stirred in Amanda a feeling that might, had her ability to empathize not been so crippled by youth and privilege, have grown into remorse for the casual amusement she'd had at her expense. But as it was, it manifested itself only as a slight feeling of disgust.

The stairs creaked and cobwebs crowded the corners of the high dark ceilings as they followed Jennifer's behind up to the second floor. Cleaning was a serious business in Amanda's house. Her mother had a cupboard big enough to walk inside dedicated to its accoutrements. There was really no olfactory evidence that the house was inhabited by living bodies at all. Which made her nose all the more keenly attuned to the smell of an unflushed toilet, say, or the sour emanations of sleep that might linger on unwashed bedclothes. She detected these things now, and other unerased traces of life, not as a powerful odour but as an undercurrent of decay, a taste of loneliness in the air. And, as Jennifer dealt with the keys, she had a sudden and awful fear that they were about to find out her life was terribly and truly hard, that something awful lay behind the door: an invalid child or parent, perhaps.

Jennifer unlocked the door and held it open for them to pass through. Amanda relaxed a little, for the room, although small and cramped, was an instant rebuff to the seediness of the communal areas and seemed almost to defend itself against them with its surfeit of polished pieces of dark wooden furniture.

Jennifer stood with her hands together, a little bird-like here in her cage. "Can I offer you girls a small glass of sherry?" she chirped.

Amanda looked at her friend and smiled. It was impossible to conceive of something so warm and syrupy when for weeks now they'd craved nothing but coldness and fizz. It was hot. They were gripped by a heat wave. They knew people who hadn't worn shoes for weeks, and others who'd taken to sleeping on the beach. The bar staff poured shandy without even having to be asked. No one, no one at all, was drinking sherry.

"Oh yes please!" said Amanda, enjoying the absurdity of it.

"Ah!" said Jennifer, pleased, and squeezed her way round to a chest of drawers on the other side of the room, on top of which sat a half-full bottle of sherry and four cut-glass sherry flutes. Slowly she poured out the burnt-coloured liquid and placed the three glasses in the middle of a coffee table that sat on stumpy leonine legs in the centre of the room. "Please, girls, take a seat," she said, gesturing to a brown corduroy settee.

Amanda pulled out her notebook and pencil from her bag and sat down. "If you don't mind, Ruth, we'll have a bit of privacy for the interview."

She didn't want her friend to forget who was the reporter here. Ruth gave her a sharp-eyed stare, picked up her sherry glass and turned her back, wandering into the corner of the room that contained the kitchen.

Jennifer sat herself down in a wing chair covered in olive velvet that was positioned opposite the sofa, on the other side of the coffee table. She crossed her legs and folded her hands in her lap.

"So," said Amanda, setting her pencil to her notepad in readiness. "What exactly happened this morning?"

And Jennifer explained how she'd been on her usual walk along East Beach that morning. It was a habit she'd started in this hot weather, getting out early on her bicycle and riding along the seafront to try and trick a little wind out of the air. She went past the boating lake and the pier and the beach huts at Thorpe Bay and on all the way to Shoeburyness and East Beach where the estuary opens out and can almost make you believe it to be the genuine sea. It was the only place you had any hope of finding fresh air these days. Back towards the town the estuary was either a seething slick of hot mud or a flat brown puddle depending on the tide, but here there was a bit of movement, little waves that came and went upon the shore.

She'd propped her bike up against the ice cream shack, closed of course at that time in the morning, and had set off on her walk along the beach. She always walked along the sand rather than the grassy bank behind in order to be as close as possible to the water. Sometimes she removed her stockings and dipped her toes in.

"Although I don't suppose your readers care whether or not I was wearing my stockings," she said, laughing nervously.

Amanda flicked her head up and, keen to maintain the feeling of professionalism her purposeful scribbles had helped cultivate, ignored Jennifer's remark. "And what time was it, Miss Mulholland?"

"Call me Jennifer, please." She reached out for her sherry glass and took a large, quite audible gulp. "Ah, yes, the time. It was around eight, a little before perhaps. There wasn't another soul on the beach. Or so I thought—"

"Yes—"

"Yes, well, I'd had a little paddle and a little sit on the beach and I was standing up just looking at the water. And then I turned round and there was a gentleman kneeling right there on the grass behind me."

"And then you saw the bird fall out of the sky," offered Amanda, a little impatient.

"Well I wouldn't say I saw it fall exactly, just that it was suddenly there. I must have had my mind on something else entirely. I thought I was on my own you see, because I usually am, and then finding out suddenly that I wasn't—it really was most odd to find a man just there behind me

30

when there was that whole empty stretch of grass. Like he was, well, waiting."

"Waiting for what?"

"I've no idea, but he was looking straight at me and for a moment I was terribly frightened—no, not frightened exactly but... it's silly I know, but I felt somehow that my time had come."

"You thought he was dangerous? A murderer?"

"No, not a murderer as such but—" she stopped, and in the silence another word crept into the room. For Amanda, for whom all sexual acts were tinged with the thrill of newly acquired experience, it carried the deepest and most exclusive of carnal frissons. For a second the room, with its many fibres—the velvet, the thick carpet, the silky tassels of the lampshades, seemed to come alive with static buzz. Maybe she had a real story here. *Attacker thwarted by falling bird.*

"Did he approach you?"

"Oh no, nothing like that. What am I saying? It's just that I can't remember actually seeing the bird fall, rather... oh, I don't know. I guess it just wasn't at all what I was expecting. Of course I soon saw what had happened. A bird had plummeted from God knows where and landed on this poor man's head."

Disappointed, Amanda floundered around for another question. "And what sort of bird was it?"

"A gull. A small gull, but still, no gull is really so very small. It did quite a bit of damage. There was blood. The poor gentleman was knocked off his knees."

"And what did you do?"

"Me? Well, once I'd got my senses together I went as quickly as I could to the phone box on Shoebury Broadway and called for an ambulance. They'd arrived by the time I got back to the poor man. Silly people thought I must be his wife. 'No,' I told them, 'no, no, I've never seen him before in my life.'

"Eccles was his name, like the cake. Raymond Eccles. They found it in his wallet, there was a letter folded up in there. Hang on a minute."

She eased herself up from the chair and walked over to a small bureau by the window. She opened it and retrieved a dishevelled-looking envelope from inside; she returned with it to her seat, continuing her story as she went.

"Right away they started shouting in his ear. 'Raymond, Raymond, can you hear me?' I think he eventually he mumbled something. I didn't see much cause to stick around after that so I left them to it. I had to get to work, after all."

Before she sat down she handed the envelope to Amanda. "Here. For some reason they handed this to me when they'd done with it and I forgot to give it back. I was halfway back across the beach before I realized I still had it in my hand. It's the letter. It's nothing personal, just a forwarding address for mail. He must've recently moved in somewhere. I'm going to send it back to him of course, but maybe it could be useful to you. It has his address on the envelope."

Amanda took it eagerly, for the question of how she was going to find out his address in order to get his side of the story had been bothering her from the beginning.

"Thanks, that's fantastic," she said, smiling at Jennifer.

"Do you want to copy it down?" she said as Amanda tucked it into her bag. "It's just I feel responsible for returning it to him."

"Oh, that's alright, I can give it to him when I go to interview him. Save you a stamp."

Jennifer looked unsure, as if reluctant to give it up, but then nodded her acquiescence—"Very well"—and returned to her seat.

"What about the gull?" asked Ruth suddenly from the other side of the room.

"Ruth, that's hardly relevant."

Jennifer peered round the wing of her chair at Ruth. "The gull? Well, funny you should ask because I walked right past it on my way back across the beach. I stopped for a moment because I noticed it twitch. It wasn't actually dead. Very nearly, but not quite. Its wing was twitching. As if, despite its sorry state, it was still trying to fly." Then she turned back to face Amanda. "I'm afraid, Amanda, I just left it there."

Three

M rs. Jean Foyle was in her front garden picking stones from the bare earth of the flowerbeds when the taxi pulled into the Close. She watched with mild interest from her crouched position as it slowly and smoothly turned the corner, and then stood up as it came to a stop outside number eight. The sound of the door opening then closing again cut through the quietness of the hot still air, and now that the taxi had pulled away she could see who the passenger had been. It was the young man who now lived at number eight: Raymond, a nephew or cousin of poor Mary Wilson's, who'd moved into the property shortly after Mary herself had left for the care home. She had, once or twice, asked him how Mary was getting on but he claimed not to be in contact with her, or with her daughter in Australia to whom he paid the rent.

He was a quiet boy, lived alone with no visitors that she'd been aware of, and Mrs. Foyle knew very little about him, apart from the fact that he had recently lost his mother. She couldn't now remember how she'd come by this information. Possibly it had come from Raymond himself, for she had welcomed him as she would have done any other newcomer to the Close, by calling with a cake and a pot of her homemade jam. But she couldn't imagine that in this doorstep conversation they would have touched on a matter so personal as a recent bereavement for, as she remembered it, the encounter had been short and rather awkward. She had put his reticence down to extreme shyness rather than rudeness and had not since bothered him with much other than a friendly smile on the occasions their paths had crossed on the street. Indeed, she would not have offered anything more on this occasion had she not been conscious that he'd seen her stand up rather purposefully when he got out of the taxi, and that they were positioned now directly opposite each other. But also there was something about the way he lingered on the pavement without making any immediate move towards his front door which seemed to invite her to cross the street. The sun was in her eyes as she did so and it wasn't until she got quite close that she noticed he had a dressing on his forehead, a square patch of wadding taped to the skin just below his hairline.

"Good afternoon, dear," she said as she approached, holding a hand up to shield her eyes from the sun.

He offered her a nod by way of greeting.

To find relief from the glare in her eyes, Mrs. Foyle positioned herself within his shadow, which fell across the pavement, causing their stances to be a little closer and more direct than they might have otherwise been.

"Are you okay, dear?" she asked, instinctively putting a hand upon his arm, for he had a most worried look upon his face.

His hand rose slowly to where the dressing was taped, his fingers rubbing lightly back and forth across its surface, a slight frown appearing on his brow.

"Was the taxi bringing you from the hospital? Did you have some kind of accident?"

Her questions had yet to be met with a response and even these direct ones were met with a silence that suggested something other than mere shyness. It occurred to her that whatever had happened to him had put him in a state of shock and she wondered why, if it was indeed the hospital he had come from, they had let him go in such a condition. He was about a head taller than her and she looked up now to try and meet his eye, but his gaze was distant, directed intently over her shoulder as if fixed on something across the other side of the street. She turned to check if there was anything worthy of his attention. But there was only her own house, her trowel abandoned on the dry grass beside the flowerbed, alongside the flowerpot in which she'd been collecting stones. She tried questioning him further:

"Do you remember what happened, dear? Did you fall? Do you remember anything at all?"

Still he was silent and she was just wondering what to do next, for it was clear to her she couldn't leave him out here on the street in such a state, when he did, at last, speak:

"Yes," he said, looking down now, still rather worriedly, into her eyes. His brow was still fixed in a frown and it seemed as if he might elaborate but again he fell silent, lifting his gaze back over her shoulder, so intently that she once again looked behind her, and saw this time her husband just now returning in the car from the bowling club. She was now suddenly impatient for the encounter to be over, for she remembered an important call she had promised him she would make and, although there had seemed plenty of time when he left, here he was already returned and the call not yet made.

She was aware that he had spoken again but, as her back had been turned and her attention elsewhere, she hadn't caught exactly what he'd said. She'd heard only the word "everything", which was to her a reassuring kind of a word. He remembered everything, perhaps, or maybe everything was okay. Either way it was enough to put her immediate concerns to rest, especially as he had now shifted his stance slightly towards the house as if preparing to enter it.

"Well, that's a relief," she said, stepping down off the pavement so that the sun once again fell across her eyes. "You should go in and get some rest now; it looks as if it might be painful."

She assumed now that the conversation was over and, telling herself that she would check on him again later, she turned to leave. But he spoke again, quite clearly this time. And what he said so surprised her that it diverted her for a moment from her impatience to cross the road and, in the years to come, was the one thing she recalled when recounting the conversation to others. Forgetful of many of her true feelings and motives at the time, she became quite proud of her own part in his story. Whether he was saying it directly to her or more to himself she couldn't tell, as her own back was once again turned. But she heard him quite clearly:

"Not painful. Beautiful."

It was this last word, beautiful, which caused her to stop. Not only because it was not a word she expected to hear in connection with an injury, but because of the way in which he said it: carefully and precisely, as if it were a word he had never said before. It dropped unexpectedly into the space between them like something fallen from the sky, making her turn back round to face him. And for a moment they both stood quite still in silence, as if examining it. But eventually Mrs. Foyle said, "Well," for she did not quite know what else to say, and the matter of the phone call had started to distract her again. "Blows to the head can make you feel awfully strange. You go and have a little lie down. I'll bring you over some soup later on so that you don't have to think about food. I made plenty yesterday, knowing that the water would be off, much more than Donald and I can possibly eat."

It was around six when Mrs. Foyle crossed the road again with her dish of tomato soup. With some effort she held one arm around it as she used her other hand to ring the doorbell. She waited but there was no answer, which was strange as she hadn't seen anyone leave the house. She thought perhaps he was asleep and this thought set her worrying, as she knew the dangers of falling asleep after a head injury. As she crouched down, putting the dish on the path beside her, she was already imagining a future conversation with someone in authority—a doctor or policeman—and how she would have to admit that she had indeed found his behaviour a little odd but had left him alone anyway. Oh dear, she thought to herself as she lifted the flap of the letterbox, she really shouldn't have done that, what was she thinking? And all because of a silly telephone call which had not been nearly as important as Donald had insisted. She called through the letterbox:

"Raymond dear, are you in there?" She put her eyes to the opening but couldn't see much beyond the hall carpet. There was no answer.

"Raymond?"

She would have no choice but to call the ambulance herself if he didn't come. She raised her voice: "It's Mrs. Foyle, dear… with the soup."

She peered in once more, and she was just about to give up and go back across the road to consult Donald about what to do next when the door suddenly opened. Mrs. Foyle fell backwards onto her hands in surprise, then quickly scrambled up, hurriedly brushing down her skirt. When she looked up she saw that, strangely, the door had not fully opened. Indeed she could not see round it at all, and it was only when she peered quite closely into the chink that had appeared that she could see Raymond, who, even more bizarrely, was crouched close to the floor just as she had been. He was looking at her, the upward glance making his eyes appear large and fearful, almost glowing in the semi-darkness behind.

"Everything okay, dear?" asked Mrs. Foyle, looking down, most puzzled.

And now, in a gesture she thought a little rude, he reached out his hand—for the soup, she assumed. She bent to pick the dish up from where it sat upon the path and having done so remained crouched, level with Raymond, as she held it out towards him.

"It's heavy, I think you might need two hands," she said, but he ignored her advice, the dish wobbling slightly as he tried to manoeuvre it around the door, making some effort, it seemed, to open it as little as possible as he did so. Once he had it inside he looked up at her again, the corner of his mouth raised very slightly in acknowledgment.

"Thank you," he said. He did say thank you.

"No bother, dear, no bother. Well, I'll leave you to your rest. Just pop the dish over when you're done, I'll—" But the door closed before she had a chance to finish.

She stood there for a moment, puzzled, the coolness of the dish, which had been in the fridge since yesterday, still on her hands. She saw something that she hadn't noticed when she'd first arrived: the curtains in the two front rooms were closed. And this settled in her mind that something odd was going on. Whatever could he be hiding in there? She turned and walked back down the path, running her eyes once more over the exterior of the bungalow as she slowly closed the gate behind her. But there was nothing more that could be gleaned from out here. She would have to talk it through with Donald over dinner.

Four

Returning home that evening after her interview with Jennifer Mulholland, Amanda retrieved the street map for Southend and its environs from its place in the drawer of the hallway table, consulting it for the first time in order to find Belvedere Close, which was the address written on the front of the envelope. Following the grid references she found it popping out like an inquisitive worm from the side of Elm Road in Shoeburyness, and, turning the corner of the page down, tucked the map into her bag, ready for the following day.

The morning was as white and dry as a blank page, the dew already evaporated from the parched grass by the side of the roads and pavements, the quietness of which was enough to allow Amanda to feel the freshness of the air even so, and a kind of virtue at being out at this hour when most were still in bed.

She decided to walk to Shoeburyness rather than take the bus. It was not a short distance and might take her an hour, but the bus involved waiting for one to arrive and she was not in the mood for that somehow. As she walked along the path that ran in front of the detached villas overlooking the estuary, of which her home was one, she saw herself from afar, as if in a film, the camera following her now as she skipped lightly down the long flight of steps that took her to the Western Esplanade, her movements disturbing the stillness of the warm morning air just enough to lift the hem of her skirt.

The tide was out and the first families were already arriving on the beach, picking their way between the broken bottles from last night's drinking and fighting that still littered the sand. Amanda skirted the boating lake and passed by the pier which, silhouetted against the low, bleached sun, seemed longer and more desperate than ever, reaching far, far out over the muddy shores like a root in search of water. She passed by the amusement arcades, flicking her hair as she did so, tousling it out behind her in a way the wind might if there were any, a gesture that asserted in some small way her difference from those few who were already loafing about in there, frittering their time along with their very average wages, as if it too were simply for spending and not for living. Such dreary pursuits were not for Amanda. She knew her family to be different. They had money. Rich: she liked the word, and had whispered it once to Ruth when, as young girls, they'd agreed to share secrets—not because she was ashamed but because she felt its power and understood it was something to be closely guarded. A small explosive thing that she carried in her pocket like a little firework, ready to burst into a shower of thrills and experiences she trusted would make way for a future beyond this town or even the comfortable wealth her parents had achieved. But Amanda being young, sheltered, and attractive, these hopes had not really attached themselves to anything beyond the city that lay twenty miles upriver, or the eligible man she felt sure was waiting there for her.

She carried on along the road, following the shell-pink curve of shingle. Beyond it, deserted dinghies sat marooned in the mud, upon which the sun lay with a kind of brazen beauty as if imploring the town to wake up, to see that the world really was wonderful. Amanda quickened her pace, feeling pretty and strangely elated, as if someone might fall in love with her at any minute.

She rang the doorbell of number eight Belvedere Close and stood waiting with her hands clasped in front of her, her mouth twitching in readiness for a smile. She noticed as she waited that the curtains were closed and realized her mistake in coming out so early on a Sunday morning. She stepped off the path to her right in order to inspect the window a little closer, for there was a chink between the two curtains. But without pressing her nose against the glass she could see nothing through it and, not wanting to be caught snooping, she returned quickly to the path. She rang the doorbell one more time and, with no expectation that it would be answered, she was just thinking how she might kill an hour or two in Shoeburyness when she noticed that the door was not actually closed. With a little push it would easily be fully opened. She gave it a very small nudge and called hesitantly through the gap:

"Hello?"

There was no reply, so she pushed a little harder, harder actually than she intended, so that the door swung completely open, although the interior was so dark it didn't initially reveal much at all. She took one step inside and peered down the hallway. Before her eyes had fully adjusted to the dim interior her nose was detecting a stale tang that could only emanate from a sink piled high with unwashed dishes, and already her mind began piecing together a picture that was fast dispelling any hopes she might have attached to Raymond Eccles—hopes that arose not from anything she knew of Mr. Eccles or from anything Jennifer Mulholland had said, but simply from the fact that he was a man and she a good looking girl and one never knew what possibilities that might present.

She called again, a little quieter this time, for she wasn't so sure she wanted an answer. But even so she took a cautious step further in, her surroundings emerging as her eyes adjusted to the lack of light. Ahead of her stretched the narrow passageway she stood in. There was a door to the left, which was closed, and a door to the right, which was open, leading to the room into which she'd tried to see from outside. Putting her head round it she began to fear she had interrupted a burglary, for the room appeared to have been ransacked. The furniture had been pulled away from the walls and formed a haphazard ring around a large disordered heap of objects, within which she could make out framed pictures, books, and ornaments. In addition to this, strewn all over the floor rather than limited to the central heap were sheets of white paper, some of which had spilled out into the hallway where they littered the floor around her feet. Looking down she noticed that they weren't blank as they'd first appeared but that each one had been drawn upon. She bent down slowly to pick one up, and it was as she did so that she noticed the man crouched silently in the shadows at the end of the passage.

Upon seeing him she was at first terribly afraid, so much so that she felt unable to move but remained frozen in a squatting position, her right hand outstretched, clutching the piece of paper she'd bent to retrieve. Crouched at either end of the passage, they faced each other. The man's wide startled eyes reflected her anxiety and slowly dissipated it, for she soon understood that he was a timid creature more afraid than she was, to be treated with caution only because of what his own fear might cause him to do next. If there had been a burglar this was surely not he.

Although their heads were turned to face each other, their bodies were oriented in opposite directions: her own towards the open door into what she assumed was the sitting room; his, bizarrely, towards the wall on the other side of the hallway. He was positioned so close to this wall that his knees were actually touching it, as if he were a child making a crude attempt to hide. She could see also that he was holding something in his hand, a thin stick-like object which he held poised like a pen but which she soon realised was actually a small plastic paintbrush. Around his feet were scattered various open tins and jars of food: jam, tomato ketchup, baked beans, salad cream. It was clear he had been engaged in some activity which she had interrupted, although he made no reaction to her presence other than to continue staring at her. She noticed now a medical dressing taped to his forehead and, remembering the accident she was supposed to be reporting on, she realized that this must be the man she was here to interview.

"Are you okay?" she asked feebly, finally breaking the silence between them. "I understand you had an accident yesterday."

Again there was silence, in which he slowly raised his left hand and touched the dressing with his fingertips.

"You have to be careful with head injuries," she said.

He looked away from her now, towards the wall, and it was only then that she saw there was something on it, some kind of substance, something lumpy, and wet, for it shone in the soft shaft of light which fell upon the wall from the dappled glass panels of the front door. Whatever it was, given the paintbrush in his hand, it was clear that he had been applying it to the walls himself, although she was certain he was not merely decorating. He had turned to face the wall now and, if it were possible, had shifted even closer to it so that his face was now within the shaft of light. He closed his eyes. Maybe it was the light that fell upon him, or the slow and precise way in which he made even the slightest movement, but Amanda could now not only see his face very clearly, but was made intensely aware of it. She stared at him, watching intently, feeling at liberty to do so, for it was clear he had slipped into a sphere from which she was completely excluded and that her presence had ceased to have any effect upon him. Even the closing of his eyes was done slowly, purposefully, as if surrendering himself to something deeply pleasurable. And the light now touched upon his lids in such a way that she could see his eyeballs trembling beneath. After a time he opened his eyes once again but stayed facing the wall, inching even closer until his nose was almost touching it. And then he moved his paintbrush to the wall, rising up a little onto the balls of his feet, with his other hand also raised, skimming the surface of the wall as if caressing it.

Amanda realized she'd been holding her breath and she let it out. And as she did so her attention broke, as if there had been a taut thread linking the two of them which now had snapped, releasing her from her absorption. She felt suddenly uncomfortable, confused, a little afraid again. Slowly she lifted herself to her feet and, without saying a word, turned and slipped back out through the front door.

Her eyes squinted shut, recoiling from the bright light, and she stumbled slightly as she made her way back down the short path to the gate. She opened it and encountered, quite alarmingly close to her on the other side, a woman.

"Are you a friend, dear?" The woman's face lurched towards her, all lipstick and wrinkles in the harsh light. She was holding out a milk bottle filled with murky water—holding it, Amanda felt, as if she might be about to smash it upon something.

Amanda blinked.

"Of Raymond's," the woman added. "Have you been visiting?"

"Oh... no," said Amanda. And then, feeling the woman's quizzical gaze still upon her: "A friend of a friend." She didn't want to explain the purpose of her visit to this woman. She was not even sure of it herself anymore.

"It's just that I'm awfully worried about him," the woman continued. "I know he's had some kind of accident and he's been acting rather strangely ever since. I don't like to pry but I popped some soup round to him yesterday and he didn't seem his usual self at all." She leaned even further forward and dropped her voice. "In fact, it seemed to me as if he was trying to hide something. Not that it would normally be any of my business but it's not his house, you see. And Mary, who owns it, is a friend of mine. I have a duty, you understand."

The short time in which the woman had been talking had given Amanda a chance to adjust, for the world to settle comfortably around her once again. The woman herself, initially so garish and intrusive, softened. The milk bottle was no longer threatening. She was simply a neighbour out watering her garden, with normal neighbourly concerns. The birds sang. A car pulled smoothly into the Close. And the sun fell warm upon Amanda's shoulders. The bright, confident ease of everything around her, the limitations of her experience, and the inability of her youthful self to really perceive what it felt, combined to disregard what she had just witnessed inside number eight Belvedere Close. She said nothing to Mrs. Foyle about what in that soft shaft of light had seemed so intimate, magical, and strange, for already her sense of it as such had all but disappeared. Instead she said: "You're right, something's not right in there. The house is a complete mess. Really bad. And he's painting the walls with something... I don't know what it is, something disgusting."

"Oh my dear!" The woman raised a hand to her mouth. "We shall have to take action. Thank goodness we have a Neighbourhood Watch meeting this evening."

"You know," said Amanda, dropping her voice conspiratorially, "I work at the *Echo*. You probably know our legal expert, Bentley? He has a column every Thursday. If you write a letter to him I'll make sure it gets published. He's always helping people with nuisance neighbours."

"Thank you dear, I shall certainly suggest it. Bentley's Legal Clinic, of course, I know it well." She looked at Amanda now with renewed interest. "You work with Mr. Bentley you say? He strikes me as such a gentleman! You open the paper and see him smiling and it's like he's smiling just for you." The woman lowered her gaze slightly and a coy smile came over her face as if Dave Bentley were flashing his grin at her right now. "You really think we have a chance of getting in the paper?"

"Of course, I'll see to it," said Amanda, knowing that being the source of a bona fide reader's letter would score her some points with the editor whose task it was to make them up each week. "My name's Amanda. Amanda Parsons. Just say I suggested you write in."

As Amanda left the Close, any disappointment she may have felt at the loss of her first proper story was outweighed by the relief of not having to write it, of being free to turn her thoughts to the evening ahead of her, and to Dirk, a tall boy with a smooth, hairless torso who was taking her on his motorbike to watch the sunset at Canvey. As she turned the corner she realized that she was still clutching the sheet of paper she'd picked up inside the bungalow. She held it up to take a look at what was drawn upon it: a simple, childish pencil drawing of a face, an oval outline inside which the features seemed strewn almost randomly. There was a lopsided kind of mouth sitting just inside the confines of the jaw line, a boxy nose positioned too high above, and two large, crude eyes, one right up on the forehead, the other in the middle of the left cheek. With one hand she scrunched it into a ball, gathering it into her fist, and threw it into the next bin she passed. Any hint of freshness that the morning air had held was gone now, the sparse strands of grass around the bin so dry and scorched they seemed to threaten fire, as if each held a little flame preparing to spark. She decided she'd get as far as the beach huts at Thorpe Bay before waiting for the bus. And as she walked, the heat of the day coiling round her limbs, she remembered Jennifer in her stuffy bedsit and thought how sad it must be to be alone.

.

Five

Those who worked on the *Echo* never considered the possibility that their words would be read by anyone outside of Southend. And by and large they were perfectly right not to. The paper was just a part of the town, like the pier, and a much more insignificant part at that. But unlike the pier, stuck resolutely in the mud of the estuary, the *Evening Echo* was occasionally presented with an opportunity to escape, usually via the commuter route.

This particular copy left on the 08:02 from Southend East in the hands of a Mr. Brian Fellen: not a regular commuter and thus not someone who had given the matter of reading material a great deal of thought, but who nevertheless grabbed the *Echo* from the hall table on his way out of the door. Once he had settled in his seat and the train had left the station, he glanced over the front page: a story about the water crisis, and a picture of local girl Lesley Ayres in her bikini, praised for shedding three stone and being now lovely enough to take the weight off any man's mind. He went no further, for he was distracted by the mist rising off the estuary as they passed by Leigh-on-Sea, and shortly afterwards he fell asleep. By the time he woke up at Fenchurch Street, the *Echo* had fallen onto the floor of the carriage and there it would have stayed, destined for a return trip to Southend, had not Mr. Fellen had a vague interest in the cricket match between Witham and Thorpe Bay, which had been attended by his son and was featured on the back page. So, keeping a foot on the paper to prevent it being kicked around by his fellow passengers as they rushed to leave the train, he sat and waited until he was the last person left in the carriage before picking it up and taking it with him down onto the Circle Line at Tower Hill.

By the time Mr. Fellen had reached the next stop, Monument, he had read all he wanted to read about Witham versus Thorpe Bay and, folding the paper in half, he turned around, placed it on the ledge behind his seat, and prepared to leave the train in three stops' time.

And there the *Echo* waited, completing an entire lap of the Circle line before it was picked up by a Mr. George Zoob, who was on his way to a meeting at the Serpentine Gallery. Mr. Zoob had a particular fondness for provincial papers, a fondness he didn't often find an outlet for in London, more often at his cottage in Norfolk, where the purchasing of the *Holkham Chronicler* was an event much anticipated by him and his wife Grace on the drive up. Indeed, the spotting of the first board displaying the *Chronicler*'s latest headline outside a newsagent was a triumphant signal that they were nearly there. Seeing the words *Evening Echo*, and perhaps also the picture of lovely Lesley Ayres in her bikini, gave Mr. Zoob an unexpected intimation of these holiday high spirits. Which is why he stood up from his seat, reached across the carriage, and retrieved the paper.

He too glanced over the piece about the water crisis and read a little about Lesley's battle with the bulge, but he knew the best bits would be nearer the back. It was the jaunty handwritten font of Bentley's Legal Clinic that made him stop at page 33, for it reminded him of the *Chronicler*'s Ask Alice column, always his and Grace's first port of call when they first sat down at the cold kitchen table in the cottage with their mugs of tea, eager to pore over the latest cleaning, fashion, and beauty tips being imparted to the housewives of Holkham. This Bentley, though, was much better looking, and George Zoob settled a little lower in his seat, crossed his legs luxuriously into the centre of the near-empty carriage and felt the beginning of a small smile cross his face as he tucked into a letter about a neighbourly dispute.

But about halfway through the letter he hit upon a sentence that changed his mood, that put him back in mind of his meeting at the Serpentine Gallery, a meeting he had, up to that point, been dreading a little, for he knew that the curator of the gallery, a close friend of his, was going to ask him for a list of artists who would be exhibiting at his forthcoming show. This he did not have. Or he did have it, but there were only five names on it. Having talked excitedly over two bottles of red wine about a groundbreaking exhibition featuring the works of British Outsider Artists he had realized quite soon afterwards that he really didn't have enough artists to put on a show of the size and magnitude they were talking about, and in the last couple of months his attempts to find more had been disappointing. But here was a sentence that gave him hope, that caused the holiday high spirits to turn into high spirits of a different kind. The sentence was this: "He has covered the walls with some kind of disgusting mural; certainly in the hall and very likely in other rooms too." That was all. But it was enough—more than enough—for Mr. Zoob to take the *Evening Echo* with him when he changed trains at South Kensington and to relay the story (with a few embellishments) to the curator of the Serpentine Gallery. And the next day he and Grace were off on a trip to Southend-on-Sea to make the acquaintance of Mr. Raymond Eccles.

Six

On Mondays Jennifer was on her own in the dress shop. Tuesdays she had Jacqueline, Wednesday was her day off, Thursdays and Fridays there was Linda, and then Rachel, the young one, helped out on Saturdays. Monday was the quiet day. On this particular Monday she'd had only three customers all morning, although all of them had resulted in a sale, which was often the way with Monday.

Her husband, Vito, was next door, which took her back to the old days when they'd first bought the two shops, both owned by Enid Scott, who'd bought them as a single premises but chopped it down the middle, taking one half for herself (Enid Scott's, the dress shop), and renting the other one out. It had been a hairdresser's when Jennifer knew it but by the time she and Vito took it over it was a florist's. Even when they'd gutted the place, the smell of chrysanthemums and wet earth had seemed to linger in the air. Mr. Cobbles opened on September 15th, 1978. The name was Vito's choice and a bad one in Jennifer's opinion, for it gave no reference to the dry cleaning aspect. Cobble & Clean had been her suggestion, but Vito had never had his heart in the dry cleaning end of things and had always wanted to be Mr. Cobbles. And Jennifer, a wife now, had taken a little pleasure in letting her husband have his way.

Now, ten years later, there were six Mr. Cobbles around and about Southend, and Vito spent very little time here on Hamlet Court Road.

Jennifer had kept the name of her shop. Enid Scott, who had been Jennifer's first boss, had not been a happy woman and death, toying with her for years while she battled one illness after another, had not been kind to her either; replacing her name with that of her former young assistant was a final injury Jennifer couldn't bring herself to inflict. The new Enid Scott's was not the same as the old Enid Scott's, however. Jennifer had had the sign repainted in an elegant gold italic script and revamped the stock, for what was the point of carrying on with lines that had proved themselves so unpopular? And she now offered an alterations service, which picked up a lot of business from next door, and bespoke dressmaking, which was getting increasingly popular; a lot of the ladies who came through the door did have the most extraordinary figures.

This morning Jennifer had walked to work with her husband for the first time in years. Steve, who managed the Mr. Cobbles next door, had been having trouble with an ingrown toenail and the other boy, Andrew, had also fallen ill over the weekend. So Vito had had to step in. He and Jennifer were each alone in their shops so they couldn't go popping next door to see each other, but that was like the old days too, and there was something different, warmer, about the noise of the machines through the wall when she knew it was Vito operating them and not one of the other two.

When she'd straightened out the changing room after her last customer and picked up a stray hearing aid that had found its way under the bench, there was a rare silence from beyond the partition. Suddenly remembering what they used to do, she went over to the wall and, reaching her free hand deep in between a row of tweed skirts, she knocked twice. She waited, her hand flat against the wall, her cheek brushed by the rough fabric, and a few seconds later her knocks were answered with two more from the other side of the wall. She smiled. He hadn't forgotten.

Then she heard another knock, on the window glass this time, and turned to look. It was one of the blond little things that belonged to Amanda Parsons. Or Mandy Matheson as she liked to call herself these days. She often passed by Enid Scott's on her way to an afternoon toddler group at the far end of Hamlet Court Road, and her acquaintance with Jennifer from the Keddies days had been enough of a foundation upon which to build a silent sort of friendship from opposite sides of the shop window. A knock and a wave and a smile and on they'd go. From behind her counter, Jennifer had watched the family grow. One little blond girl had soon become two, then three, and now four, each identical to the last.

But today, after the knock, the bell rang and the four little blond things ran in as though unleashed into the wild, immediately hiding and giggling in between the racks of skirts and blouses and summer jackets. Their mother walked directly to the counter, and Jennifer walked over to it too, positioning herself behind it just in time to meet her there.

"Jennifer Mulholland!" It was a long while since Jennifer had seen Amanda at such close quarters and she noticed with surprise how her face was gathering detail around the eyes, how they'd sunk just enough to make you wonder what life was like in there.

"Can't stay," she continued, casting a half-hearted glance around the shop to check the whereabouts of her children.

"I just had to come in and tell you what I saw in the paper yesterday." She reached into her bag and pulled out a couple of torn-out pages, patting them clumsily down onto the counter. "It's him," she said with a firm, final pat. "Ray bloody Eccles!"

A moment to breathe, and then she carried on:

"He's an artist! And... and look! It's you!" She tapped her finger insistently upon the page. "That day you saw the bird falling he, well, God knows what happened, but it's you, Jennifer! I'm sure of it. You see, there you are, right here, can't you see? And no one knows but you and I. And Ruth Smithson I suppose, wherever she is. Listen here, it says... well you read it, you just read it. Penthouse on Green Park, his own show at—I don't know, one of those big London galleries. Shacked up with a cheating no-good bitch but— imagine, just imagine, when he saw you on that beach he saw straight into your soul. It was... oh, you know, one of those moments, like a bright light shines and everything comes together. It's what we're all waiting for, it's—" She paused for breath once again, her eyes scanning the pages as if she might find the word she was looking for there. "Anyway, I can't stand here chatting all day, but you read it. You read it and then you get in touch with this journalist, this Lucy person, and tell her who you are." She bent down and scooped up the smallest little girl—a child of around two—who had arrived by her knees. She hoisted the child onto her hip and smoothed her hand over the fine blond hair which, having gathered a static buzz among Jennifer's stock, stood up like a dandelion clock around her little head. Amanda leaned in and whispered across the counter. "You *inspired* him, Jennifer, who would have thought it? If only we'd known. *I* could have written this, this could've been my big break, and you, well, you could be having tea at the Ritz, and—well it's not too late," she said, patting the pages down firmly on the counter. "Here's your chance."

Jennifer found herself adrift, quite unable to think. In search of something to cling to she found the child. "Hello treasure," she said, touching a finger against her soft, flushed cheek.

"Say hello, Samantha," said Amanda, standing upright again and smiling. "My little angel. They're all angels, but... oh, they grow up so fast, I..." She sat the child on the counter and glanced quickly over her shoulder. "You know, Jennifer," she said, lowering her voice and leaning in once more, "there comes a time in life, don't you think? It kind of creeps up on you, when you start to suspect you're not quite as marvellous as you once thought. I mean, that maybe nothing that great is going to happen. That life is just going to... well, *carry on*. I think it was then that I started to think it would be nice to have a child. Oh, it's wonderful, it really is! I mean, look at her, she's perfect, they're all perfect, but... oh, I don't know what I'm talking about. You read this article is all I'm saying." She looked down at the paper. "This doesn't happen to everyone, Jennifer, that's what I'm trying to say. On posters it says, and mugs—your face, Miss Mulholland, on a mug!" She prised the child's little fingers away from the edge of the page. "Don't do that sweetie, please don't do that, you'll tear it. Chaos wherever we go!" Amanda laughed wearily. "Where are those little angels of mine?" She looked over her shoulder again. "Girls!" Then turned back briefly to Jennifer. "Half term. Horrible. We really should go. But you read it, Jennifer, you'll see what I'm talking about." She picked up Samantha and turned towards the door. "Come on girls. I'm counting to three.

One... two... th—" The little blond things scurried out of their hiding places and grabbed onto various parts of their mother, the whole ensemble shuffling sideways out of the door. "You, Jennifer, are a great big mystery!" Amanda called over the jangle of the bell. And then they were gone.

Jennifer stood there, a great big mystery, staring out over the small expanse of her shop. Her eyes dropped to the newspaper on the counter below, not focusing, noncommittal, and yet she could hardly help certain words lurching out at her: Ray Eccles; artist; Southend-on-Sea; 1976. She ran her hand over the surface of the paper, smoothing it, listening to the dry sound it made in the silence. There was a grainy reproduction of a painting, a portrait, and she traced her finger round and around the shape of the face. "Me," she said quietly, and the word wriggled down deep into her belly. Maybe it really was her face; she could see that it could be. And yet it was utterly strange. Looking at it she felt the utter strangeness of her own being, straining feebly to make itself known. The fibrous contents of her shop— so much wool and linen and cotton—seemed a dry and tangled trap around her. But here was a face that opened up a space above her head that was cold and vast, like the sky over the sea. Her gaze floated up to the top of the page and she started to read.

Half past four, and teatime at the Ritz is in full swing. The gilt-festooned Palm Court is alive with the tinkling cacophony that accompanies this afternoon ritual: silver teaspoons clinking against bone china, the trickle of tea falling from the pot in an elegant arc, the pianist putting the ivories through their paces, and the lilting cadence of laughter and inconsequential chatter. It's all so English that most people here are American tourists. The last place you would expect to meet two luminaries of the contemporary art scene, the outsider art scene no less, which professes to trawl its artists from the very fringes of society, casting its net among mental institutions, urban slums, and prisons. And depositing them here, it seems, in London's most expensive district, if the experience of Ray Eccles is anything to go by. For it is he I am here to meet. He and Grace Zoob his... minder?... dealer?... lover? It's a question I mean to address later.

The Ritz is what Ray Eccles does on a Friday afternoon. We are sitting around the Zoobs' table, kept for them on a rolling booking. It's in the corner, because Ray likes corners, and his seat faces the wall, because he likes to face a wall rather than a room full of people. Grace orders a pot of Darjeeling for three along with "the works" from a tall, equine, French waiter. While we wait I ask Ray how he likes the picture on the wall in front of him, a rusty-haired Renoir nude; reproduction, I presume. "She looks sad," he says and Grace quickly nods in agreement. "It's true—so sad, and yet it's something no one ever says about Renoir. There's something in the soft application of paint, as if one were looking at the painting through a great wash of tears. Of course there's sadness in Ray's paintings as well. In every painting I think, by virtue of its being... well... just a painting."

In Ray Eccles' case, "just a painting," or a group of paintings, has been his ticket to, if not superstardom exactly, then recognition by the art world establishment. His work is currently on show at the Hayward Gallery alongside that of some of the century's major British portrait painters—Freud, Spencer, Hockney—which is the first time an outsider artist has been placed alongside mainstream artists in a major exhibition. Eccles is far from sidelined. He is placed as an *equal in the lineup. Indeed it is his painting,* She *(which is the title of all of his paintings), from which the exhibition takes its name, and it is the image of this unnamed woman, staring out with an expression both enigmatic and revelatory against a backdrop of sea, that is the "face" of the show, plastered on Underground posters, on the banners that flap outside the gallery in the Thames-side breeze, and on the postcards, prints, and mugs on sale in the shop.*

His prominent inclusion has not gone unopposed by some critics, who claim there is a whole sea of difference between the works of recognised great artists and those of so-called outsiders. But the show's curator, Sarah Dixon, vehemently defends Eccles' right to be here. "This show is looking at how the artist has obsessively portrayed particular muses over the centuries, and Ray Eccles' She *series represents the most extensive study of one female subject in the whole of contemporary art. He may not have had the training of a fine artist but his work shows incredible skill and sensitivity, as well as an understanding of composition and the viewer's relationship to the work, something that is often lacking in other outsider artists. Outsider or not, Eccles is a great artist of our time and fully deserves to be represented here."*

Our waiter returns with a tray and deposits tea, hot water, milk, all in gleaming silver receptacles. He then brings a stand laden with scones, miniature cakes, and crustless sandwiches. A smile spreads across Eccles' face and he dives shamelessly for the most indulgent confection of chocolate and cream on offer. He has a kind, quiet face, a complexion whose clarity and pallor seem to speak of a life spent indoors and which, were it not for the delicate latticework of wrinkles encircling his eyes, would seem unnaturally youthful for a man who has just turned 52. His hair is thick, dark, short, worn in a neat side parting, and his clothes—a dark pinstriped suit, white shirt, and blue tie—utterly conventional. It is the uniform of the city worker, although, having nothing of the bullish air that usually accompanies it, Ray Eccles could never really be mistaken for one of that breed. I shrink from calling it innocence—the likening of the outsider artist to the child being a rather trite observation—but there is something about him that cries out to be loved. Not admired, or applauded, but simply loved. It is undeniably endearing and, suddenly infected with the thrill of this teatime treat, I too bypass the cucumber sandwiches and head straight for the chocolate.

He and Grace make an odd couple, if couple is the right word. An art critic colleague, hearing that I was conducting this interview, described Mrs. Zoob as "scary" and "thin." Both are true, although her short, spiky silver hair, thin lips painted a bright scarlet, prominent cheek bones, and relentlessly black attire seem softened just by virtue of being next to Ray—and perhaps by the presence between her fingers of a scone laden with clotted cream.

The two came together in 1976, at a time when Grace and her husband George were assembling their collection of outsider art, now by far the biggest and most important in the country. Quick definition of outsider art for the uninitiated (though definitions aren't easy here): it is art by those who do not see themselves as artists, untrained and urged to create by something other than a desire to exhibit or to achieve recognition. A less kind definition would call it the art of the insane, which outsider artists commonly, though not exclusively, are.

In the early '70s, George Zoob was a struggling young gallery owner occupying cramped quarters in Marylebone who had become captivated by the art of non-artists and decided to dedicate himself to giving them a platform in the UK. One day, in swept Grace Harrison, daughter of an American cookie magnate who had been in London since the mid-60s. The two married in '73 and, with Grace's money behind him, George began amassing a collection in earnest, travelling the globe in search of the mad, bad, dispossessed, and talented. He came upon Ray after spotting a letter in a local newspaper, Southend-on-Sea's Evening Echo, that detailed a neighbourly dispute, the menace in question being a chap who was disfiguring the walls of his rented home with a mural and generally causing the property—owned by an elderly woman living in a nursing home in Cumbria—to slip into a shoddy state of disrepair. "George was just overcome by the feeling that he had to go and visit this man, that he could be creating something truly extraordinary," says Grace.

"This man" was Ray Eccles, a man who had been working until that point as an admin assistant in the offices of Southend District Council, and what he was creating was indeed something pretty extraordinary. When Grace and George arrived in July of 1976, Eccles had covered almost every inch of his small suburban bungalow—walls, ceilings, doors, everywhere—with pictures of a woman standing on a beach, the same image over and over. Perhaps even more extraordinary were the materials he had used—biro, pencil, and crayon in some places, all naïve though unremarkable choices, but in others he had painted with food—the hotpots, stews, soups, and casseroles that were delivered on a daily basis by members of a neighbourhood watch committee intent on seeing just what he was up to in there. "He just used what he could get his hands on," says Grace. "When he ran out of pens and pencils he started painting in food, *and, sometimes, when he ran out of that, he even used his own blood and semen." Ray tucks blankly into a mini Victoria sponge during this explanation of his first foray into painting, seemingly unembarrassed and uninterested. It is very hard to reconcile the clean, be-suited and—I give up—innocent man beside me with this picture of a crazed, masturbating visionary defacing the walls of an old lady's bungalow. "Didn't it, you know, smell a bit?" I ask Grace, who looks offended by the question. "We didn't notice anything like that. We were overcome by the beauty of it. There was something in those faces so deep and soulful and true. We were just astonished, totally astonished."*

What happened next not only saved Eccles from the wrath of his neighbours but saw him transplanted from his sleepy Southend suburb to the centre of London's wealthiest neighbourhood. Grace and George offered £20,000 cash to the old lady in Cumbria, a figure way above the market value of her home, and took possession of the place. In the early months they invited friends and enthusiasts for visits, but as the work began to degrade they acted to preserve it, coating it with preservative and covering the walls with light-proof fabric. "We've had a few problems with squatters but the neighbours keep an eye on the place for us," says Grace. "I think they like having it there, it's something special, secret. When Ray had his first show at the Serpentine we arranged a minibus to bring them all to the opening night. They loved it. We employ a gardener to keep the garden looking nice, and we repaint the windows every so often. From the outside it looks like any other suburban bungalow."

"And do you have any plans for it? It seems a shame to have it just sitting there."

"No, not at the moment. To be honest we like having it there, just for us. It preserves the magic of the discovery, a little part of Ray's genius that's not available for general consumption. We sometimes go there, take down the sheets, and just marvel at it."

"And Ray?"

"No," she says, looking across at him. "No, he wouldn't want to go back."

So the art-viewing public have had to content themselves with somewhat smaller masterpieces: the sheets of paper torn from notebooks that were filled up before the walls were attacked and which were the stars of the Zoobs' first Outsiders show at the Serpentine Gallery in 1976, and, later, the more conventionally sized canvases that Ray has produced since, of the sort currently exhibited at the Hayward.

Eccles, left without a home, went to live with the Zoobs in their penthouse apartment overlooking Green Park, less than 100 metres from where we are now. He was given one room as a studio and Grace set her friends to work on a soup production line to ensure him a steady supply of "paint."

I do wonder if the whole food thing hasn't become a bit of a gimmick though. Eccles didn't choose to work in those materials to begin with: he just used them because they were all he had available. Why didn't the Zoobs, when they were able to, provide him with proper, quality paints to work with? "We did, of course," says Grace, "and he uses those too. But there's something about the food that conventional materials can't replicate. We had to admit that the raw power of the work was, in part at least, attributable to the materials. It's not up to us to dictate what he uses; he makes his own choices." And it helped to get the work noticed, surely? "Yes, maybe," Grace concedes, "but a reputation can't be sustained *on soup alone!" She laughs, a surprisingly melodious sound, and I realize that Ray has hardly spoken a word, that we've been discussing him as if he weren't here. I turn to face him and ask him what made him start painting in the first place. What makes an admin assistant wake up one morning and decide to start drawing, and to carry on drawing in such an obsessive fashion?*

"I just felt like I had to," he says. It seems like the best I'm going to get, but then he carries on: "She told me to."

"She?"

The question of who exactly She is has been left unanswered and many, I suspect, would like to keep it that way, as it helps to cultivate an air of mystery. Grace certainly looks at me suspiciously when I say, "And who is she?"

"The woman on the beach," Ray answers. It seems for a moment like I might actually get somewhere.

"Do you know her?"

Eccles is silent.

"Is it your mother?"

That She is Ray's mother, Nora, with whom he lived until the age of 39, caring for her through a long illness until her death in 1976, is a theory that has been put forward before, and certainly seems the most likely explanation. But Eccles looks me straight in the eyes and says simply, "My mother is dead," and I decide to give up this line of questioning and move on to something equally delicate: the nature of the relationship between Ray, Grace, and George.

Although the Zoobs' marriage appears to be very much a reality, they've never been afraid to "extend the welcome," as it were. George's sexual history is particularly labyrinthine and, throughout the early years of their marriage at least, he took a whole string of lovers, both male and female, while

69

Grace too had her share. "We don't feel as if we own each other, if that is what you mean," she says when I ask if she would describe their marriage as "open." Things no doubt calmed down a bit as the years rolled on but it's no secret that a fair amount of bed-hopping goes on in the penthouse round the corner, something that came to the fore six years ago when Grace gave birth to a daughter, Mira (after Miró, her favourite artist), and wrote an article in a national newspaper stating her indifference as to whether the father was George or Ray. Both men apparently remain ignorant (as does Grace) as to which of them is the biological father. "We all love, care for, and look after Mira. It doesn't help to start labelling people—this man is your father, this man is not. I don't know myself and I don't care. There is nothing sordid or even particularly unusual about the way we live. We eat breakfast together, we go for walks, we make and display and collect art—there is a lot of love in our house."

One cannot help but think, however, that one member of this merry threesome is rather more vulnerable than the others. I turn to Ray, intending to ask him how he feels he fits into the family, but just as I do so Grace reaches across to him and wipes a small smudge of cream from the corner of his mouth, and the gesture is so tender that it seems to validate everything she has just said about love and respect and normality. I keep my mouth shut and Grace calls the waiter over for the bill.

I'm invited back to the apartment to view the collection and take a look at Eccles' studio. This is where it all began, at the top of a modern '60s apartment block, 23 St. James' Place, which for years was Grace and George's main exhibiting space. The collection—continuously growing and developing—still crams the walls, and yet more pictures are *stacked up against each other along the skirting boards. The Zoobs still see the apartment very much as a gallery; anyone can view the collection by appointment and there are frequent visits from outsider art scholars and enthusiasts. Grace talks half-heartedly about finding a permanent home for the work at one of the major galleries—the Tate already houses a small number of Eccles in their permanent collection and there has been talk of them taking on the entire Zoob collection—but there is something of an "after we're gone" feel about this plan. For now the Zoobs seem happy to be surrounded by the work here in their home.*

She points out some of her favourites: Willie Macbean's dark, angry, wide-jawed figures depicted with ferocious strokes of charcoal that practically tear at the paper; Fay Nelson's delicate plant-like forms which, upon closer inspection, reveal more ominous imagery lurking within their feathery fronds—wide eyes, tongues, genitals; Zenith Pool's insect sculptures made from pieces of scrap metal and interlocked in a great warlike—or orgiastic—throng. There's more, all intense, energy-filled, intoxicating stuff, and I can see exactly why this type of art and its creators have captivated the Zoobs for so long.

But at the end of the day it's just madness, is it not? One big, uncontrolled, psychotic splurge of the unconscious onto paper. The pictures all have an inwardness that repels as much as it intrigues the viewer. There is no awareness of "us," the consumers of art. These pictures were not made to be seen and they allow no dialogue. Is that art? It's a debate that could run and run, but not one it's easy to have in relation to Eccles, whose work, although sharing some of the characteristics of outsider art—an obsessive repetition of the same theme being the most notable one—could never be described as anything less than art. His paintings have balance, poise, composition, and, most importantly, a relationship with the viewer. His woman—whoever she is—looks at us and we look at her, and we see not only her but ourselves too. She asks us questions about love, loss, sadness, truth, humanity. "I am not like them," said Eccles in reference to his fellow outsiders in an early interview, conducted at the time of the 1976 show at the Serpentine Gallery, "because I paint what is real. The others are making it up, they are lying."

Although a number of the Zoobs' artists have gone on to enjoy considerable commercial success (the Nelsons in particular fetch large sums at auction) the art world seems to have siphoned Eccles off into a different realm. "Would you include Ray's work if you were to recreate the 1976 Outsiders exhibition?" I ask Grace. "That's not something we would ever do, but I see your point," she says. "Labels—outsider art, this art, that art—are helpful to a certain extent, especially if you are trying to get work noticed, but ultimately they break down and we should be thankful for that. It's not surprising really, because the 'group' is something imposed from the outside. They are not a group, they are a collection of individuals producing very different work; of course they are going to go in different directions. Is Ray still an outsider artist? Yes, and no, it doesn't matter—he is an artist."

We go into a vast sitting room with a row of huge windows overlooking the park, where I meet George, sitting feet up and knees apart in underpants and a white shirt, reading a newspaper, and Mira, playing quietly on the floor with the contents of the cutlery drawer. She's made a neat bed for the whisk and is holding two forks up on either side of it. "They're nurses," I'm told when I enquire. She's an unbelievably beautiful child: thick, dark, curly hair and *elegant, delicate features which make me suddenly aware of their counterparts in Grace, revealing a similarly rarefied, if hardened, beauty in her too. I cannot help but switch my gaze between the two fathers, trying to work it out, although, bizarrely, I can see something of each of them in Mira's face.*

We leave them to it and go on up to Ray's studio. I am expecting the usual: white walls, paint-splattered floor scattered with dirty rags. What I get is a room covered with Ray's mysterious vision, every inch of wall filled with that same face in its perennial seaside setting.

"We whitewash over all this every few months," says Grace. "I know, it breaks my heart too, but it's something we've had to get used to. He can't work in an empty room; he must be surrounded by this. But he's never satisfied; he continually wants to start over again, so that's what we let him do. We'd never be able to supply him with enough canvases or have space to store them all. Believe me, it's the only way."

I look up, and around, and about, understanding something of the wonder Grace and George must have experienced when they first entered the Eccles bungalow all those years ago. Not that I haven't seen it all before. The same woman, the same sea, the same sky appears in all his work, and here they are again. But each time I see them, I see something new. I don't mean a new element—a new patch of light in the sky, a new colour in the subject's eye (although these things do change)—but a work that seems wholly new. How Eccles manages it, I can't begin to explain, but each of his paintings reminds me that art, at its best, is a direct, sensuous response to the world and each one offers that response as if it were responding for the first time—and we, as viewers, are somehow forced to do the same. Taken objectively the scene is not even a particularly compelling

*one. A woman stands on a beach. Not a beautiful beach,
not a particularly beautiful woman. There is no beautiful
play of light in the sky, or upon the quietly swelling sea. And
yet... beautiful is the only word I can think of to describe it.
The world restored to glory in the quietest, most mysterious
of ways.*

*There is, at the same time, something curiously dispas-
sionate about the work. The response is direct, yes, but not
emotional. For works essentially primitive in their execution,
this is unusual. His brush seems to make each element more
itself than ever—capable, like a word perfectly expressive of
what it describes, of unlocking some secret of the thing it
touches. The sea is exactly sea, the sky exactly sky, the grass
exactly grass, the woman exactly woman. Who is she? Does
it matter? I'm starting to believe it unimportant. She is both
no one and everyone. She is exactly and completely herself.*

*

Jennifer looked up. Here she was, in her shop. The silence
was heavy; the street seemed to have emptied out in a
way that made her wonder if she'd missed something,
some catastrophe. But then a lone car drove slowly past
and, as the sound of the engine receded, she caught the
distant judder-judder of machinery making holes in the
road somewhere, and now a woman walking past, a child
running on behind, and she breathed again, relieved, and a
little disappointed too, that the world was carrying on. The
day she'd seen a seagull fall on the head of a man called
Ray Eccles seemed impossibly remote, the memory a mist
around her mind in which she flailed about for a moment
trying to grab at least some recollection of his face. But

it was too late, for any traces that remained had already been replaced by the photograph in the newspaper: this man, this *artist*, who, sitting strange and aloof in his studio, made her feel indignant, violated, when what she'd been beginning to feel was *special*, that being alive amounted to something, that she was unique, that she had something in her worth capturing. All those crazy, illogical, unarticulated hopes that as day followed day she didn't dare give space to, for they were obscured and discounted continually by the plain undeniable facts: of her aging body; of her trivial thoughts; of her petty successes and failures; that one day she was going to die. But this little picture in the paper, this knowledge that someone had seen and held her in their mind, this proof that she existed, that something had passed between two people, dared her to hear another voice. A voice which whispered to her: *you will never die.* So, so quietly it whispered to her, but loud enough for her to think just for an instant about doing something rash. The article mentioned a gallery, the Hayward; she knew the name of the couple too, Zoob; there were four trains going to London every hour of the day. But… she walked over to the full-length mirror, feeling suddenly curious, as if it might at last have something new to tell her. *Fluttering in the Thames-side breeze.* That was a nice and peculiar thing to think about. And her reflection seemed to respond, leaf-like, to waver a little, as if with another gust it might blow away and be gone. And then what would she see?

She and Vito walked home together along the seafront. It was the long way round, but the knocking on the wall seemed to have lodged in Vito a mood of nostalgia and he had it in his head that he was taking her for a Rossi ice cream. It was the first day after the clocks had gone forward, the first long evening, and whereas yesterday this hour had been marked by a dull and deepening gloom, the sun was behind them now, on its way down, and the warmth hit their backs as they walked, hand in hand like one of those sweet old couples still in love. The tide was high and Jennifer looked far across the water to the long low rise of Kent. Across the mouth of the Thames. She never really thought of it as that. The sea, the estuary, the water, but never the Thames; as seemingly unconnected to the knotty nucleus of London as her own breath to the dark and intricate interior of her lungs. She took a breath now, a big one, for she felt somehow thin, dispersed. On mugs. On posters in the Underground. On banners that flap outside the gallery in the Thames-side breeze. She clung tighter to Vito's hand to anchor herself here on the Western Esplanade. She looked at him, at his face, at the dark little eyes that sat deep and secretive in his skull, and not for the first time found herself surprised—at her life, and this man beside her, who was her husband.

"What a woman!" he said, turning to her, an attentive crumple on his brow. "She knock twice, knock knock, and I know she thinking about me." He smiled—and grabbed her suddenly under the chin in the rough affectionate way he had with her, his kiss on her cheek dry like a child's. "My Jenny, working away for a no-good husband like me." He liked to call himself no good, although really she couldn't have hoped for any better.

She'd met him not long after the pier fire of 1976. The day they'd let people back on, the two of them had made the mile-long walk to the end together. By that time their friendship had got them as far as a trip to the pictures and a meal at his brother's restaurant but had not yet presented them with such a blank stretch of time as this. As Jennifer had cast her eyes down the long bare planks of wood tapering off into the distance, she'd thought maybe it hadn't been such a good idea. But off they'd set. The summer had finally relented and the breeze gave some purpose to their steps, a little movement to their silence. Jennifer had found herself recalling the fire, the raging ball of heat she'd watched from the window of her bedsit, rolling on the water as if the sun had fallen. It had seemed to presage not disaster but something wonderful, caught up somehow in the centre of that bundle of fire. As she and Vito had neared the end of the pier, now a confusing tangle of blackened, smoke-diseased beams—well, it was the usual thoughts about dreams going up in smoke. And it was at that moment he decided to kiss her, the first time their lips had met. She hadn't seen it coming, hadn't wanted it either, not then. But she had accepted it all the same, and the silent seal it gave to their union.

"Next year I take you to Positano!" he said now, freeing her grandly, and she smiled because she'd taught herself to appreciate the promise of it. She knew it was never going to happen but saw it more as a figure of speech, a way of expressing himself when life was suddenly beautiful. "I love you" was not something he thought necessary to keep repeating. But "I take you to Positano" was his way of saying the same thing.

"I can just see that happening with your mother here," she said, and she hated the sound of her voice, the school-mistress tone she took with him.

La Mamma was coming to live with them and she was coming tomorrow. Her whole life until now had been spent in the village in Calabria where she was born. But she was old, and the hills were steep. Her husband had died and her two sons left for England long ago. So she was coming to live with Jennifer and Vito and cried every night on the phone because she didn't want to.

They reached the blue and white awning of the Rossi ice cream parlour and joined the back of the queue of people waiting for scoops of vanilla or lemon ice, the only two flavours offered out here on the street. For the more exotic sorts you had to go inside and order from the bar. They bought two cones of vanilla from a skinny, freckled girl with rolled-up sleeves, and weaved with them through the cars parked two-deep in the middle of the wide Esplanade. On the other side of the road they sat side by side on the low wall overlooking the beach and the water, their feet skimming the shingle below. Vito put his arm round her, gathering her to him as if he knew instinctively that he might lose her if he wasn't careful—on a sudden breeze or a rash surrender, which might take her drifting out over the water.

They sat in silence, their old comfort blanket. In the early days, conversation in English had been a struggle. Silence, by comparison, was a solace, and lying back in it together a kind of addiction, persuading them that they could communicate on a deeper level. Sometimes it felt like they could, as if something were really happening in the silent spaces between. At other times it was just as if they had nothing to say. And she felt it now, this closeness and this distance, their unique capacity and complete inability to communicate.

He squeezed her shoulder: always his touch was just a little too much, and made her stiffen and flinch when she wanted only to soften. She felt, in its tenacity, a sudden sense of their freedom disappearing, of his mother's impending arrival, and in his smile, when he turned to her, a twist of regret, as if they'd never really discovered what that freedom was, or how to use it. She'd felt the same thing, the looming of a great bind and change, an anxious kind of joy, when she'd been expecting their child.

A baby! She'd thought herself too old for that kind of thing. And she was, as it turned out. It had died inside her before she'd felt any sign it was alive. Never before had she felt the desire for a child, but afterwards it burned through her whole body. They'd tried again but there'd been no more babies. The loss was too much to talk about. And now La Mamma was coming to them to die.

"Look at him!" said Vito, nodding at a gull standing flat-footed on the sand, its head cocked, its cruel eye turned upon them. "He knows. He knows, don't you fella? He knows more than you think, Jenny. They're not dumb, these birds."

Jennifer looked at the gull, and it looked back, as if waiting for her to say something. Did he really know?

Vito knew all about the birds. And the fishes. Any creature you like: giant squid, water buffalo, hippopotamus. He filled his spare hours with nature programmes. The long evenings were one vicious mating ritual after another. The world around them was erupting in fertility: dense schools of fish, skies brimming with birds, insects writhing and squelching in the rich mulch of the rainforest floor. Jennifer kept one eye on it all—on little slimy sacks of glue-eyed young and dominant males locking horns—while she sat in her chair knitting teddies for children in Africa.

Vito kicked his foot out and the gull flapped and hopped and then took off across the beach and out over the water, letting out a high, shrill cry. Jennifer followed it with her eyes, watching its wide white wings rising and falling in long, powerful strokes and then stretching out, perfectly still, as the bird soared and glided in a slow diagonal across the blue sky.

Their house was up on the Cliffs. They weren't cliffs exactly—rather higher ground that gave a view over the sea—but hills weren't common in Southend so they tended to make a fuss over the few there were. At the top were the tea gardens and the bandstand, and then the park descended in tiers, with winding paths and a set of steps offering long and slow or short and steep routes down to the Esplanade.

The best houses were to be found looking out over the water along the Royal Parade: tall and elegant with lead-roofed verandas and wrought iron balconies. Theirs wasn't one of the best houses, but it was a good house all the same, located just round the corner overlooking a well-tended square. With just two bedrooms it was not large, but it was certainly big enough, and in their ten years of marriage they'd had no reason to move. When Jennifer had moved her furniture in from the bedsit she'd felt at last it had found its rightful home, and this alone was enough to validate her decision to marry. She polished it almost daily, just as her mother had always done right into old age, and allowed herself to feel a little smug towards her elder sister, whose offer of the furniture after their mother's death had always felt like an insult, knowing as she did the cramped conditions Jennifer had been forced into. Rosemary had disappointed her. But how could she argue? Her sister had a family; Jennifer was alone. It was enough, in Rosemary's mind, to give her a right to move into the family home, casting Jennifer out even after all those years of caring for their mother.

Jennifer sometimes felt that she and Vito should have done more to make the house their own. It was only this year, in preparation for La Mamma, that they'd done anything in the way of home improvements, converting the dining room into a downstairs bedroom and adding a little lean-to extension to house a bathroom. The outside, though, had always been well kept, and Jennifer got a little pleasure from returning home each evening to the prettiest house in the terrace. There were window boxes filled with red geraniums running along the sills of the bay window, three white hydrangea bushes whose pom-pom flowers clustered along the top of the low front wall, and six neat, well-swept steps leading up to the front door, which were going to pose a problem for La Mamma. They'd had handrails put in last week: thick tubes of pale grey steel that made two institutional flat-topped arches on either side of the steps and announced to their neighbours they were making allowances, accommodating. Jennifer sometimes passed such houses, hidden within a normal terrace but with some little touch like these rails, or lettering on the windows, or a sign staked in the front garden: something that marked them out as not a house at all but a dental surgery or an old people's home or a nursery.

Inside, they peeled off into their separate routines of a normal weekday homecoming: Vito upstairs to change and Jennifer into the kitchen to start the dinner. The evening sun was stretching through the window above the sink on its final long, low burn, the light as sweet and sticky as the remnants of vanilla ice cream on her lips. She felt a little drunk. A giddy kind of feeling as if the world had loosened its grip, letting her reel a little, unsupported. Her life felt suddenly light around her shoulders, as though she might wriggle out of it. She wasn't sure she liked it. She'd always enjoyed the feeling of being held in: a good secure waistband around her stomach, a buttoned-up tailored jacket, tightly laced shoes. Marriage, she always thought, would feel much the same: like a well-fitting skirt suit. At the best times, it did. How appropriate and valid she sometimes felt when, moving about the kitchen, say, she remembered herself a wife. But she found there was still plenty of room inside for loneliness, for regrets.

But marriage to Vito was an unexpected thing to have happened, a thing she often reminded herself she should be grateful for. It had taken her places she'd never expected to go. To Italy, for a start, although she'd seen nothing of it but Vito's hometown of Stilo. Twice a year they caught a plane to Lamezia Terme and drove across the toe of Italy, through the mountainous forests of Calabria where short men foraged for mushrooms and kidnappers hid their victims. Jennifer caught glimpses of the sea from the windows of their small rented car before they descended deep into the valley where Vito was born. And for two weeks she ate pizza and drank strong, sweet coffee and felt more keenly than ever the absence of children as the women around her gabbled their dialect and eyed her with a puzzled expression as though they couldn't quite see the point of her.

The people of Stilo were short and old and suspicious, the vegetables dark and shiny and lush. The streets so narrow you could walk down the middle and, stretching out your arms, touch the buildings on either side. The afternoons so hot you had to shutter yourself inside and sleep. Sometimes she ventured out in these dead midday hours, the clatter of plates like the rattle of bones, and those who stared out from the darkened doorways and shady street corners—the very old and the very young, the dogs and the donkeys—did so with such direct, unflinching eyes that she felt herself invisible. Now and then a brass band would strike a mournful note through the afternoon, drawing the living from their cool tombs to follow another of their number to the cemetery, which grew and prospered at the bottom of the hill.

In the evenings—every evening—she and Vito took a stroll up to the Basilica, a tiny Byzantine chapel surrounded by cacti and scrawny chickens, and watched over by a thin and silent man whose cigarette stubs gathered in the dusty earth outside the entrance. As she stood at the top of the hill looking down on the crumbling stone maze of streets and alleys that had kept her prisoner all day, and the bells of the domed church below tolled out across the desolate valley, something seemed to gather and rise from the town, which revealed it in that instant not as a dying place, but one more deeply alive than she had ever known. She didn't belong there. She had no point. And yet she felt there *was* a point. In Stilo—this forgotten, faraway little place—there was a point. There'd be no more reason to go there now that La Mamma was coming to Southend.

She filled the kettle to boil water for the pasta, poured olive oil into a pan and set garlic frying over a low heat. Then she went to check on the room they'd prepared for La Mamma. They'd bought a new pine set—a single bed, bedside table, chest of drawers, wardrobe—and on the low surfaces Jennifer had laid out the white crocheted cloths she was sent each Christmas from Vito's cousin. They'd had the room papered in a pretty rose sprig, and a border with larger, fuller blooms went round the room just above the picture rail. Tomorrow she would pick flowers from the garden and put clean towels in the little ensuite, another place where handrails had been added. But for now she just sat down on the bed, feeling the springs give way beneath her. She moved a little, up and down—*bed hopping*—and let her mind slip its moorings, float downriver past art galleries and penthouses filled with paintings (of her!) and a lot of love, until the smell of garlic from next door brought her back to this little pink room. A sudden tightness about the ribs, and with it a vague intimation of her first solitary moments of married life when, lying in the dark with her husband a steadily breathing presence beside her, she'd felt a sudden and frightening dwindling of possibility as, above, she saw the sparks of other selves and lives and loves, only then revealing their existence as they wheeled and eddied off into the night like tiny squealing fireworks.

"So—" began Vito, plunging his fork deep into his bowl of spaghetti. Jennifer recognised it as more of an audible setting to task than a prelude to conversation and, sure enough, the fork was loaded, lifted to his mouth, taken out clean, and plunged back in the bowl without another utterance. He was immediately absorbed in his eating, busy and content. She wanted to say something. She picked up her fork and paused to try and catch his eye across the table, giving him the chance to look up and see that something had happened today. She wanted to share it with him, and yet keep it secret too. If he could just notice a change in her, maybe that would be enough.

"Amanda Matheson came in today," she said, for she thought suddenly of the little girls whose blond heads, like spume upon the waves, rose in her memory as expressive, somehow, of her giddy, weightless feeling. "With all four of the girls," she added.

"Four she got now?"

"Yes, four," Jennifer said, trying not to be disappointed with him. "Samantha and… oh, I forget their names but they're little angels, all of them."

"Did you burn the garlic?"

"A little, maybe."

"You got to watch it. Don't take your eyes off it. I know what you're like. You have the flame too high, and then you go wandering off. You just need to melt it, *very* gently, gently, and don't—"

"Vito?" she said firmly, and waited for him to stop eating and look up at her.

"What? What is it, Jenny?"

Why couldn't she *say* anything?

"Did I ever tell you I was once the Southend Carnival Queen?"

He laughed, not unkindly. "I think that was a long time ago, Jenny."

"Not so long! I can still remember it. I can still remember it like it was yesterday," she said, speaking quickly, trying to generate some real feeling. "They had the final in the Odeon. Me and five others. Derek de Marney was the judge—you must know Derek de Marney? He was the first truly handsome man I'd ever seen in the flesh!" She laughed, trying to manufacture the excitement, the glorious warmth of winning. But all that had stayed with her after all these years was the press of the Mayor's belly as he led her in the first dance at the gala ball, and little Robert Ferris, with whom she'd ended the evening, letting him touch her breast through the thick white satin of her dress. She said:

"When they called out my name I could hardly stand for happiness!"

Vito had at last stopped eating. His cutlery rested on the side of his plate and his attention was turned upon her face.

She met his eyes. "Do you think I'm... nice to look at?" she said quietly.

"I think you're lovely," he said. "The most lovely thing in the whole of Keddies, remember? That's why I picked you. Straight off the shelf. Hey, what's the matter?" He reached his hand across the table in search of hers. "You're a silly thing. You know what? I'm going to buy you a present."

She laughed.

"No, I mean it. I'm going to buy you whatever you want. You name it. Anything. Venice? You want to go to Venice? I'll take you to Venice. I've got the money, the money is no problem, we've got more money sitting around than—"

"Vito, I don't want anything."

"There must be something."

"No, really, the only thing I ever wanted was—"

"I know, you want to go to Positano, but I think Venice would be more romantic. Won't you come with me to Venice?"

"Vito, your mother is coming to live with us tomorrow."

"Yes," he said, and sighed. "Poor Mamma." And that was that.

"I've done some chicken if you want it," she said, gesturing to the hob where a few flat pieces of breaded chicken lay waiting in the frying pan. "And there's salad... on the side."

"Yes," he said distractedly, for he'd noticed the time on his watch. "Do you see? It's eight o'clock already. We're missing the dolphins, Jenny. Your favourites. Let's take it in front of the television tonight. Come on, special treat."

Seven

This Saturday, as for the last five Saturdays, Grace Zoob was walking her daughter to the studio on Bruton Place to have her portrait painted. It was a group portrait, Mira just one of an ensemble. "Oh, but the most important one, my darling," Grace told the child, who by now, at the sixth sitting, needed a little persuading.

They held hands as they waited for the green man at the crossing beside The Ritz on Piccadilly. Mira called the green man Ray and the red man George: "Because the green man is moving and the red man is lying down."

. George was in one of his holes and spent a lot of time in bed.

"Bye bye, George," she said, waving at the traffic light as they set off, quite sprightly, across the road.

There'd really been no need to wait. It was early, and even here the traffic was still sparse. The one low red car that did approach as they hit the middle of the road came to a slow and satisfied stop as if pleased at the interruption: a chance to break, look around, move the gear stick, rev up again. The sky was a cold, clear blue. The streets were empty, the buildings tall, and Grace Zoob felt that way too: tall and empty, like something made of glass. Sometimes it was a joy to be empty. To hold that clean space inside your stomach that came from being out and about before breakfast. It made her feel so light and so powerful. She had an inkling she might just become something marvellous were she never to eat again.

They crossed onto Berkeley Street and Mira ran on ahead, her shoes patting against the pavement like peals of laughter. The light was so crystalline, Grace fancied she could see the thread that linked them, sticky and glistening and bowing in the morning air. She never felt more connected to her daughter than when she watched her from afar like this, as if the little girl were her own childhood self, still there, running on ahead somewhere in the pure, sunlit distance.

Mira stopped at the bottom of Berkeley Square and the two of them walked on together, hand in hand once more, past the Bentley showroom. The cars inside were so dashing with their grinning silver grilles and devouring eyes, ready at any moment to pounce and shatter their plate-glass cage. And next door a shop selling crumbling ancient art, with always a big smooth-eyed Buddha in the window who looked at her in an entirely different way: he sat back, knowing, knowing something secret, something hidden. She was only waiting for the day that would send her through one door or the other to buy something: a Bentley or a Buddha, she didn't know which.

And then round the corner into Bruton Place, a tidy back street of small-scale studios and warehouses. Even the vans which came to collect and deliver were toy-like, always clean with well-painted lettering on their sides as if taken fresh from the box.

The studio was number 37 and Grace lifted Mira so she could ring the bell. They were buzzed in and climbed the narrow wooden stairway to the first floor, where the door was open and opera poured lavishly out onto the landing. Gregoire, the bastard, was standing behind his easel at one end of the room. He ignored them as they walked in.

The room stretched across the entire top floor of the building, but this was a small building and so the room was not large. There were metal-framed windows at both ends, bare floorboards, a large potted plant in one corner, and a wooden bench across the centre. This was the setting for all Gregoire's portraits, so potently familiar that the room now had the feel of a painting itself: the dirty, scuffed-up floorboards as if textured with oil paint, the plant's smooth leaves streaked with brushstrokes of green, even the sky outside the window, so clear and pale it seemed still wet.

The other sitters had arrived already. Two women and two men. They loitered separately around the walls, bending and stretching as if gearing up for a dance class, all keeping their distance from the bench, whose narrow hardness would soon bore into their spines for three long hours. Grace had plenty of friends who'd sat for Gregoire; she knew of its crippling boredom. She'd sat round dinner tables and been the only one not able to throw her head back and remember the pain. "Oh the ache," "the ordeal," "the boredom of sitting still," "—and naked! I was a nude of course, weren't you?" It seemed a decadent kind of boredom, an exquisite kind of pain, and Grace so wanted to know it too, but she had never been asked to sit.

Gregoire had done George of course, in the early '70s (George was terribly pretty in the early '70s). She'd seen the painting only a couple of times but there was a book at home with a reproduction spread across the centrefold. She didn't know what made her open it out so often, for it only gave her a stab to see it: the languid twist of his limbs, the worn-out flop of his penis, the pink bloom across his chest...

Grace knelt down in front of Mira, unbuttoned and removed her coat, and smoothed her curls away from her face.

"Are you alright, sweetie?" she said without concern for the answer, wanting only to say something. The beauty and perfection of her own child was frightening at times. How close and how distant she was, her eyes dark and secretive like closed little sea anemones. She felt a pang—how cruel it seemed that they'd ever been parted. Nine months she'd waited to know what it was growing inside her and when it arrived—this living thing that breathed and moved inside its own little universe—she realized the time of closeness and of knowing was already lost.

Her hands slipped down over Mira's narrow shoulders. Tiny, bird-like bones she could crush with a firmer grip. She'd often thought of doing so. Or strangling, smothering, drowning. What thoughts! Her hands carried on down over the dry, coarse netting of her tutu. "The child can wear what the fuck she likes," Gregoire had said, and Mira had chosen this: a greying, moth-eaten, ill-fitting item that had been donated to her fancy-dress box from the wardrobe department of the English National Ballet. It was far too big for her and the leotard hung loose over her flat chest, the faintly soiled crotch sagging and gaping beneath her own tight and innocent sex. Grace had made her wear a red polo neck underneath for warmth and to fill her out a bit, and on her feet she had a pair of red Wellington boots, which were Mira's own choice of footwear. Today being a cold day, spring not quite having conquered the frosts, she'd worn her green duffel coat over the top on the way to the studio which, sticking out over the tutu, had made her into a neat little cone. As they left the house Grace told her she looked like a Christmas tree, which had made her smile and helped to shift the last traces of her temper. She'd fallen out of love with the tutu and had wanted to wear her pyjamas instead. "You can't switch now," Grace had said, forcing a stubborn woollen leg down into the tutu as it kicked and twisted. "You've made your choice and you have to stick with it."

Grace looked up again at the other sitters. The man with the dry, untidy beard and mustard shirt who would not stop licking his lips; the other man who was younger, considerably so, and had arranged himself elegantly against the wall, his back slightly arched, his palms flat either side, one foot raised upon the wall, and his thin features turned upon Gregoire, who pretended not to notice and carried on mixing his paints.

The women matched the men in age. The older one wore a loose jersey dress that suggested a body underneath so soft it might be possible to knead it into another shape entirely. She hung down to touch her bare toes, and the gape in the dress as she did so revealed large, pendulous white breasts that elongated away from her body like lava in a lamp, as if she were morphing already. The younger, in contrast, was as boned as a corset. She wore a neat, black shift that finished above the knee, a smooth black bob that finished just below the jaw, and a pair of shiny black high heels that sounded out hard and hollow against the wooden boards as she paced back and forth in front of the far window.

"You're the prettiest by a million miles," Grace whispered to her daughter.

Gregoire coughed and the four responded, gathering quickly on the bench like birds huddled for warmth. This was how he wanted them: bunched uncomfortably in the centre rather than spread out more evenly along its length. Grace kissed Mira on the forehead and watched her run over to take up her position, which was lying on the floor at one end of the bench, removed from the other sitters by a distance of at least a metre. She lay down and was immediately still, her eyes suddenly vacant, as if dead.

Grace stood near the door with her hands in her pockets watching the group gel and solidify into a single entity, lifted and bound by a silent camaraderie and a secret knowledge of themselves as Art. And feeling her own irrelevance, her own lightness of being off the edge of the canvas, she backed out onto the landing, turned, and made her way quickly back down the stairs and out onto the street.

Something always happened between going in and coming out of the studio: a waking up, an arrival of life upon the streets. The stillness shifted and the new air, churned up by exhaust fumes swirling round the Square and the movement of people in and out of doors, always helped to buoy Grace on to the next part of her day—and today, she suddenly felt sure, would be the start of something marvellous. And as if to celebrate, or to encourage it in some way, she decided to buy something lovely. Something for Ray. He'd seemed a little melancholy recently, a little… but why did one always need a reason to buy presents? She walked to the end of Bruton Place and followed the road round into Bruton Street, the home of Patisserie Marie. There she bought six of Ray's favourite strawberry tarts and, leaving the shop with a large white box and an appetite for shopping, set off for Jermyn Street to buy him a tie.

For ties it had to be Christopher Earnest, for he sold nothing but silk ties, and besides, it was her favourite shop in the world. A secret little place tucked off Jermyn Street; she often felt she was his only customer. Certainly she'd never met anyone else in there, and when she came through the door Christopher Earnest would look up with an expression that said, "Ah, madam, *here* you are," as if he'd been waiting for her all morning.

He was a strange creature, a puppet, brought to life by the short discreet ring of the bell as the door opened. And small, so small as to appear more than just small, but rather scaled-down in some peculiar way.

In she stepped, onto the plush green carpet that was a bed of moss across the floor, so lush that she felt in danger of sinking a little too deep if she stayed in one place for too long. There was a large crystal chandelier, a dazzle in the centre of the room, and all the ties were arranged around the edges in their own individual wooden compartments, rolled up to look like gigantic boiled sweets.

"Ah," she thought, taking it in, standing just inside the door. She stayed there for a moment, scanning, waiting to see what would draw her attention, and to her left a band of silvery weaves flashed at her like coins in the sun. She moved closer and there was one that stood out, with threads of gold, yellow, silver, black, and turquoise woven together in a way that resembled a mackerel's belly. She would take it.

"If I may say so, you've chosen the most beautiful tie today, madam," chimed Christopher Earnest when she took it to the counter to pay.

Every choice she made here was the best possible choice, every thing she picked out the most beautiful thing.

"If I may hold it up to the light for you, madam, you'll notice... ah! Do you see?" He held it up to the chandelier and sure enough the threads sparkled as though woven through with light. It was the face of Christopher Earnest that suddenly struck her though, caught in the creamy glow. His features were so delicate, held taut and poised upon his face: the nostrils fixed in a constant flare, the mouth curling at the corners as if pulled by strings. So pale he might have been pickled in a jar. And yet at his eyes, collected along the pink rims and sparkling even more than the golden threads, were little pools of tears. It was a thing as surprising as seeing a statue weeping.

He put the tie on the counter and could no longer ignore the tears, for as his head lowered they threatened to spill and trickle down over his cheeks. Reaching underneath, he pulled out a perfectly pressed white handkerchief and, flicking it free of its folds, dabbed it along his eyes. "I do apologize, madam, I must confess I'm a little tired today."

"Oh?" she said quietly, coming closer to the counter, her movements small and slow as if drawing near to a wild animal. He looked up at her and she saw that his flower-like features had been dislodged, that they trembled as though touched by a breeze.

"I—" he began, and she withdrew, suddenly terribly afraid that he was about to confide in her, for she had glimpsed, as their eyes met, the taint of tragedy in his face— the pallor of the skin, the crêpey folds around his eyes. Petals on the turn. The thought had come to her that he was dying, and then she felt it with certainty. Christopher Earnest was dying. And she was dying too. She felt it not abstractly, but physically, a terrible pit in her chest. For one horrifying moment she couldn't find her breath—so she laughed, forcing it back, and he coughed, then lowered his eyes towards the counter, his hands reaching underneath for a bag, resuming the transaction.

She took her purchase in its small bag and left the shop, wanting now only to be home. The day was filling up. People were out, doing things and seeing things. On Piccadilly the tourist buses were revved and waiting, bodies were pouring out of the Underground like sand through an egg timer. Hurriedly she entered the park, keeping to the wide path that ran down the eastern edge, and then slipped into the dark passageway that dipped below her apartment block and took her to the entrance on the other side, on St. James' Place. The lobby—cool, marbled, bare—was always a refuge of sorts, and she stood there for a moment letting the thick, solid walls subdue her jellied flesh. And as she stepped into the lift she felt a small sense of victory, of death's shadow lifting as she ascended smoothly to the top floor.

She unlocked the door of her apartment and, without taking her coat off or putting down her bag, walked quickly across the hall and stood in the doorway of the sitting room. There he was: her angel. She always hoped for more when she crept up on Ray like this, to catch something, some glimpse of his secret self, or even to find him floating or glowing, some outward indication of the inner worlds he sailed through. But still it was magic just to watch him when he did not know himself to be watched. One could love someone very easily that way.

She did wish he wouldn't stand so very close to the window though—like a moth worn out from bashing its head against the glass.

What a funny creature he was. And George too. How had she ever ended up here with the two of them?

Her great-great-grandmother had supplied hand-baked cookies to her local store. Her great-grandfather had the first small factory. Her grandfather built a worldwide cookie empire. Her father inherited it and drank a lot. And she, his last born and least loved, had only wanted to *do* something, something not made of butter and sugar and chopped-up nuts. Something not made of money. And yet there was nothing she seemed very good at doing. Maybe it wasn't about doing, just being. Being with the right people. She'd gone on protests. To underground poetry performances in freezing, disused factories. She'd moved in with a woman, convinced it was the only way. But... maybe she could have chosen better. And then she'd found George, who lived in one room and ricocheted around it like a squash ball, a compact reactive thing lacking the protective casing that allowed most people to move through life absorbing its everyday extremes. Once she'd been in that room with him for a while, it was strange, all she wanted was to go back and be in it with him a while longer. This world he'd unearthed of outsiders, of maniacs and madmen and gentle geniuses and art that could not be stopped, even if you shut your eyes and your wallet—it was so very different from biscuits, sold in boxes, millions of boxes every single year.

She had all this money, you see. Not a fortune, but a dull, lifeless burden all the same: every day like something she'd bought off the shelf, overprocessed and bland. What a sweet thrill to surrender it to George and watch it come alive in his hands. He didn't make things with it, or even buy things exactly, but he transformed things. He turned perfectly worthless creations into masterpieces, perfect nobodies into artists. And it wasn't magic, or a con, just an ability to see things others couldn't. A fresh and penetrating gaze. This was art and beauty and life in its purest form. Extracted like gold from the earth, unrefined and raw. The rest was just more biscuits in boxes. How it frustrated him when others couldn't see it, when reviewers talked endlessly about the funny old street cleaner who lived with his dear old mum, as if the miracle was not the work itself but that such a creature should respond to the world at all.

To be honest, Grace found it difficult herself. She wasn't an explorer like George. She saw the pettiness of life and longed to rise above it but… well, it wasn't to see art and beauty and life in its purest form that she accompanied George to Southend-on-Sea in 1976. They'd been in the middle of a heat wave in the middle of a city. The chance of a sea breeze, her toes in the water, and some titillation from a small-town neighbourly dispute were what had persuaded her into their hot little car that morning.

Her skin had felt as if it was melting into the car's black plastic seats as they'd made their way out of London to the east. Out on the highway the sun made puddles on the tarmac, and the land on either side, brown and hedgeless, slipped hypnotically past. She'd been asleep by the time they reached the outskirts of the town, but as they drove deeper into the smallness of suburbia she woke, wallowing in a warm, sexy somnolence as she looked about at her new surroundings. Here, among the mini-roundabouts, the driveways and kiddies' bicycles, her life seemed a most unusual, beautiful thing. She had a beautiful, unusual husband, a beautiful, unusual home; she really was rather unusually beautiful herself, she thought, catching the angle of her sweat-defined jaw in the wing mirror.

"Let's have a baby!" she said, turning lazily to George, and he smiled at her, reaching his hand around her thigh in a way that made her feel skinny and sexy.

They found the road easily enough, a small cul-de-sac of bungalows, and picked a door upon which to knock. A woman answered, only moderately elderly, but settled already into the clothes, the hairstyle, and the lipstick that would do for her until the grave. Grace adored her; she was perfect. Number eight, she said, was the one they were looking for, her lips pursing as she pointed opposite. "Are you from the council?" she asked, and George said, no, they were art collectors, giving her a small smile and a gentlemanly bow of gratitude before setting out across the road.

There was no answer at number eight. All the curtains were closed. "Let's go, honey," said Grace, kissing George's earlobe and glancing over her shoulder. "Number Twelve is still standing there," she whispered into his ear. "She has her arms folded and she's looking very suspicious. I think we should go before she calls the police." Grace laughed, taking George's hand, but he slipped it free and started making his way around the side of the bungalow. She waited for a moment and, not knowing what else to do, followed him round, finding him with one foot inside the back door.

"George!" she said, running over and taking his hand again.

"Hello!" His shout disappeared into the house. There was no response.

"Honey, come on. Let's come back later. We can walk down to the beach from here. Ice cream?" She tugged on his hand to persuade him out but he pulled back, stronger, taking her in with him. They stood together in the empty kitchen. The lino was sticky under their feet. The whole room felt sticky. Ahead of them, a dense trail of ants made a pilgrimage across the worktop to a spilt dollop of tomato sauce. The air felt heavy, as if something awful had just happened. "It stinks," said Grace.

George moved slowly deeper into the room and, still clutching his hand, Grace followed on behind, stopping by his side in the doorway through to the entrance hall.

"There you go!" said George, whispering now, letting go of her hand and stepping forward.

The light was not good in the hallway. To begin with, Grace sensed rather than saw what was around her. The silence teemed with unseen life, as it might in the middle of a jungle. She too walked onward into the space, and slowly the dark shapes upon the walls took form. She could discern a face, a woman, and around her a kind of landscape. She moved a little closer. It was not a naturalistic figure, not accurate or clear. Obscured somehow by the thickness of the paint or... what was it? She reached out her hand. It was grainy to the touch, dry and chalky, coming off a little on her fingertips. Grace had her face close to the wall now, close to this other face. Not real... and yet curiously and intimately recognizable. Like someone half remembered from a dream. A face that awoke something in her, like a deep nostalgia. It was a reticent beauty, the figure seeming to withdraw back into the wall, her eyes looking both inwards and out, as though beckoning shyly, wanting to be followed, to reveal something... some secret thing. Grace turned, disturbed by the sound of George's feet on the carpet, and was met by the same figure again on the opposite wall—not dryly repeated, like on a sheet of wallpaper, but as if truly there anew. Everywhere Grace moved her gaze, there the figure reappeared, as if she was a projection of her own imagination, her own yearning.

"It's amazing," she said, looking for George, wanting to know that he was seeing it too.

"Come on," he whispered. "There's someone here."

As she moved towards him Grace could hear a soft, scratching, shuffling kind of noise coming from across the hallway. George started towards a door, and she followed slowly on behind. Slowly, he nudged it open—just a small way before it was blocked by a bed. But there was enough room for the two of them to peer round and see, in the far corner of the room, a small crouched figure, his face close against the wall as if communicating with someone just the other side. And all around, the same beautiful dark cloud of angels, as if he were whispering them into existence. So this was it. The source. This little rabbit.

*

Look at him—he really hadn't changed at all. How strange that some people could not stop creating things, whereas others couldn't ever seem to start—always, always Grace felt she was just about to. One only had to put canvas under Ray for him to fill it up, and one had to, really, for otherwise it would come out anyway, all over the floor or the walls and make an awful mess. It was terribly infantile. Terribly... pure. Like a spring upon some secret mountaintop, out it came, crystal and cold. What happened to it further down the valley—how it was received and by whom—was of no concern; that little spring just kept on. What was driving it? Why the same scene over and over? Grace had never asked him who the woman was. Because in some strange and mysterious way she believed it was herself.

"Dearest!" she said, advancing from the threshold.

She put her bags down on the glass coffee table and went to him at the window, touching a hand to the back of his head. "I've bought you fruit tarts and a new tie—just wait till you see it, it's the most beautiful thing you ever saw, and Christopher Earnest, he… the poor man was completely broken from tiredness and emotion. I was quite moved by it. I think I might… I don't know—write something!" And immediately as she said it she knew she never would.

A sudden emptiness arrived, something incredibly sad. No victory after all.

But things came and then they went and one simply had to move on.

"What was that, dearest? Did you say something? Were you asking about the painting? Gregoire's painting, you mean? How sweet of you. Well, to tell the truth, I haven't seen it but I expect it shall be wonderful as usual. He's surely sleeping with that young woman—that always sets up a bit of tension. You see, dearest, what Gregoire has discovered is that if you sit four people close up next to each other and ask them to sit still and keep silent for hours at a time, they all start falling in love with each other. It's all too obvious: the old woman is in love with the old man; the old man is in love with the young woman; the young woman is in love with the young man; the young man is in love with Gregoire. Ah-ha! But Gregoire chooses the young woman—Gregoire can choose who he likes. And that's where it starts hotting up. Jealousy happens." She raised her hands on either side of her head and wiggled her fingers, which was the jealousy, happening. "Oh it all shows beautifully in their faces, all that love and jealousy fizzing around. The tension—so subtle. The critics don't know how he does it. Easy: he shags his subjects and paints what he sees."

Ray turned to face her. Dear one, had he actually been listening?

"What about Mira?"

"Oh, Mira!" Grace laughed. "Don't you worry about Mira, dearest, Mira's just there to balance out the composition, make it less neat. A little question mark lying at the foot of the bench. Who is she? Whose is she? A little tutu-ed angel, they'll say, cupid in galoshes. The beloved irony."

His face was baffled, a little wounded, as it always was by such talk. Grace could talk about art, that was one thing she *could* do. What else was there to do when its burning centre eluded one?

But she didn't like to see him wounded. She loved him. What a strange and wonderful thing: she really did love the little rabbit. She opened the box containing the strawberry tarts and held it under his face. "You want one?" she said, and he smiled and nodded. She kissed him on the mouth and stroked a hand over his cheek, soft and soapy-smooth. "Come on then."

They went through to the kitchen and she placed two tarts on two white plates, setting them down on the table and herself on the chair alongside. Ray sat opposite with his hands on his lap, waiting. The strawberries sat fat and pompous in their bed of custard, indecently red, the glaze like molten glass over the top. They seemed to defy her to eat them, such haughty little things. And yet she would, whether they liked it or not. That was the pleasure in it, to dig one's teeth in and show them who was boss. And how softly they yielded. Such a crush of sweetness and softness in her mouth.

"You wait till you see the tie I bought you, dearest," said Grace, a little afraid that the mackerel-belly sheen of the silk had dulled in the bag. But when they'd finished eating she unwrapped it from its tissue paper and laid it out upon the table, and if anything it was even more beautiful here on its own, spread out between them as pointless and pleasing as a length of ribbon. Ray ran his finger down over it, right down to its pointed end.

"It's like—"

"A fish?" she said, eagerly

"Yes."

They'd had the same thought. And with it another new thought swam into her mind. It was the thing she'd been waiting for all morning, all her life maybe. The thing that would save her. But she waited a little longer, watching it grow and take shape as she slipped the tie around Ray's neck. She fixed the knot, smoothed the silk down over his chest and then looked up and said:

"I've had a marvellous idea!"

She got to her feet. "I want you to paint me. I want you to paint me for the new exhibition." Her body felt suddenly alive and supple again. She walked quickly round to the other side of the table and leaned over it, her palms flat upon the surface. She considered the elegance of her arms, imagined the shallow swoop of her back. "Let's give them something different this time." She moved back over to Ray, kneeling down on the floor in front of him. "Let's start soon," she said, trying to find his gaze. "Let's start tomorrow. You will do it, won't you dearest?" She kissed him. "Oh I knew that you would! You do know I love you, don't you?" She laughed. "I can hardly wait to tell George." And she laughed again, throwing her head back now, enjoying the long stretch of her neck. "Not that he'll give a shit! Have you seen him this morning? Oh dearest, I just know it's going to be marvellous. Dear George, I should go in and see him. See if there's been any progress."

Grace called it the ninety degrees of depression. George's bouts always started here, at the lowest point, which was flat on his back, and then he would rise up a little at a time: a few pillows under the head to begin with, and then he'd be sitting up in bed and then in the armchair downstairs and eventually he'd be standing and walking and laughing again and they'd all of them go up to Norfolk for a holiday.

She ran a glass of water from the tap and laid out four water biscuits on a clean plate, spreading each thinly with butter. She carried both out into the hall and down to George's room at the back of the apartment, tapping gently with her knuckle on the closed door. She opened it slowly, balancing the glass on the plate, entering George's dark and stagnant den.

"Oh." His voice quivered weakly across the space between them. "Is that you, dearest?"

"No, it's me," Grace whispered, shutting the door behind her. "I came to see you."

The curtains were closed and she stood still for a moment while her eyes adjusted to the low light. There was never much in here anyway, or in any of the back rooms overlooking St. James' Place, a tall and narrow back street into which the light trickled thinly if at all. The wide views over the park from the front were startling by comparison and George complained it was not good for his health to be always having to adjust between the two, coming out of these dim, intimate back-spaces to be hit anew by the giddying expanse of green, and a fresh and reckless desire to throw himself out the window.

She walked over to the bed and looked down at the pale, bearded face that lay there.

"Poor Georgie in his hole and no one knows how to get him out of it," he said, his voice slow and deep as if rising through a more viscous medium.

She put a hand to his face and felt a small surge of pleasure and relief to be near a thing so resolutely human as George. Ray was always so far away. George, at least, was down here with her, with his thick, dark hair and rich mushroom smell. She loved to bury herself in his chest, like burrowing into wet earth; the first time they'd made love she'd known that at last she'd found somewhere to plant herself.

George said it was a hole, a hollow, empty, lifeless thing. But to Grace, depression was just another lover that he took to his bed. There was no need for it, in her opinion. One simply had to make the decision to get up and get on with the day, if that was what one wanted to do—she sometimes wondered, though, at her own ability to do so, as if she might have missed something, some terrible truth that had passed her by.

She often felt these small deficiencies. She blamed George and the conditions he'd imposed upon their union. That they should be free. Free to explore other people, other possibilities. It was such a bind, forever trying to find someone to explore. It presented such endless opportunities for failure. Wasn't it the point of getting married that one could forget about all that? Just settle back and relax for a minute? When she'd become pregnant… well, there at last was a chance. Why let George assume things? Maybe it was Ray's.

"Ray's?" George had laughed and laughed and laughed. "Well, good old Ray." Couldn't he have been just a little bit jealous?

She bent to kiss him, entering his warm, yeasty microclimate.

"I've brought you some water biscuits," she said, making room for them and the glass of water on the bedside table.

"Ah, yes, water biscuits! Water biscuits cure all ills. You used to give me love, Gracie, and now you give me water biscuits. Horrible, dry, barren things that clog up my throat." He turned his head in the direction of the plate and made a sour face. "Oh, you've buttered them today, have you? You must be softening a little."

"Poor George," she said, stroking her hand over his damp, clammy forehead. She'd learnt that to wait, and to say such things, was the only way.

"Poor George," said George in reply, closing his eyes and letting himself be stroked. "Poor George."

They were quiet for a while and then George rolled over, turned away from her. "Grace?" he said.

"Yes, George?"

"Will you give me a cuddle?"

She walked round the other side of the bed, slowly took off her shoes, and slipped in under the covers. The stale heat and mulchy smell was an obscene pleasure to her washed and clothed body that had recently walked out across Berkeley Square in the cold morning air. Mira—she suddenly thought of Mira, lying there in her tutu and red galoshes at the foot of a wooden bench. She turned, giving her back to George so that she was the one to be held. The single bed forced them close together as if they were sheltering from some danger. He pulled her to him, pinning her arm against her side, and she felt his breath on the back of her neck. Strange, it did feel awfully lonely to be held sometimes—because you were never *entirely* held. There was always some part of you that was left untouched.

Eight

"Come in, dearest."

Ray was standing timidly in the doorway. George had asked to see him, as he sometimes did, and Grace must have sent him up. He walked slowly across the large kelim rug that filled the space between the door and George's bed.

"Here," said George, patting the edge of the bed.

Ray sat down cautiously, knees and feet held tight together, hands clasped upon his lap. He was dressed in a thin white T-shirt, a vest maybe, with a silk tie around his neck. It had flecks of silver, blue, green, and gold in it, quite beautiful. George reached out a hand to touch it but, unable to muster the energy to reach that far, ended up stroking the air just in front of it. Sometimes he felt that seeing Ray might make him feel better.

"Tell me something, Ray. Tell me... tell me about the sky."

Ray closed his eyes.

"What colour is it?"

A slight frown appeared upon his brow as if he was straining to see behind his closed lids. "White," he said, without opening them. "Pink. Blue. Grey. Green—" He stopped, and was silent for a moment. "White."

"Like... smoke? Milk?"

"Milk," he said uncertainly. "But sort of... fizzing."

"Quivering? Like a pan of hot milk on the cusp of coming to boil?" George took Ray's hand, felt maybe they were getting somewhere, starting to see the same thing.

"No. It's more like sky," said Ray, withdrawing his hand.

"What about her? What's her face like?"

"Like an angel."

"Her eyes? What colour are they?"

"Gold. And blue. And green, and—"

"Like your tie." George touched it this time, and smiled. "And her skin?"

"Smooth. Dusty. Speckled."

"A pebble?" He liked that, he could feel its dusty smoothness, see the mineral salty specks.

"Maybe."

"Her lips?"

"They're open. She's talking to me."

"The barriers thrown aside, the promise of intimacy … " George closed his eyes for a moment. "Is she lovely?"

"Yes."

"*Very* lovely?" said George, who could not imagine a face so lovely and yet wanted to, desperately—oh, how he longed to see it. "Tell me."

But it was no good. Ray couldn't describe her; George should know that by now. And even if he could, George would never truly be able to see what was in his head, or even to imagine it. But if only that were possible, if only he could escape himself for a moment. See something new. Something beautiful. It was so wearisome being himself all these years. His flesh hung so heavy on his bones, like great lumps of clay crudely slapped on. One shouldn't have to suffer it for a whole lifetime. Being oneself, and then just … not being oneself. Not being at all. It seemed so limiting, so unfair somehow. It didn't make any sense.

"Have you ever thought about painting something else, dearest?"

"Something else?" Ray opened his eyes. "Like what?"

"Oh, I don't know—" George looked about him vaguely, and then gave up, for what else was there, really? "I just don't know how you keep going." This was the thing that really puzzled him. How to keep going?

Ray looked at him, uncomprehending. "I can't stop." His hands were fidgeting now, the fingers twisting and turning about each other on his lap. His shoulders twitched, his feet moved in shuffling little circles on the rug. George knew he wanted to be gone, to get back to his work. Oh, to feel such urgency, such compulsion.

Then he felt Ray's finger touch lightly to the back of his hand, which rested palm down near the edge of the bed. He knew at once what he was doing: he was drawing on it. George closed his eyes and tried to see the line in his mind's eye, to follow it, make sense of it. But he soon lost it and it became simply a path, one that led with reassuring purpose over the veins on the back of his hand, then over his wrist and up his forearm. He felt, under Ray's touch, the dryness of his bones, the sickness of his soul, and longed to be healed, to be made beautiful again. For a time he felt it really might be happening. The tingle of his skin waking up, the attention of that roving finger fixed so intently, so lovingly, upon his limb. But then he opened his eyes and looked at Ray. He'd slipped to the floor and was kneeling beside the bed, bent close over George's arm. He really was beautiful. The frown was gone, his face intent and peaceful, like a Botticelli angel. And yet that loving attention which

George had felt focused upon himself was a lie: Ray was clearly elsewhere. If there was a movement of love then George was irrelevant to it. He was simply a canvas.

With more strength than he thought he had in him, he jerked up from his pillows and seized Ray's head in his hands, pulling it upwards to meet his own face and pressing his lips to Ray's as if it might be possible to insert himself forcibly into the flow. Ray stood up immediately, removing himself from the kiss, and stumbled towards the bedside table, bumping into it with enough force to dislodge an untouched bowl of lentil soup that Grace had brought up earlier. It fell to the floor and the soup splashed over the rug like vomit.

Nine

Vito's brother, Paolo, was bringing La Mamma from Stilo. He and his wife, Giulietta, had been there all week helping her pack up, which was their end of the bargain. "We do our bit, don't you worry," Paolo had said, a hand on Jennifer's shoulder. He had a notion that having La Mamma here in England would be no trouble, great fun, just like the old days when he and Giulietta had first opened the restaurant.

Vito had spent his first months in England at the sink in The Amalfi. And even by the time Jennifer met him, when he'd finally found a job at a cobbler's on Southchurch Road, he was still elbow-deep in soapsuds at the weekends. Jennifer liked the feel of his hands, waxy and plump. She liked his small, well-polished shoes too. And the way words stumbled out of his mouth in surprising combinations. She wasn't sure about love but she thought she could do a good enough job of looking after him—until he spat out her macaroni cheese and sent her to his sister-in-law at The Amalfi for cooking lessons. Jennifer disliked Giulietta back then. She was small, silly, and always pregnant. But it didn't take Jennifer long to see she didn't have such a great time being married to Paolo.

They were good times, really. Paolo and Giulietta were still living above the restaurant and the four of them would sit around and sip Amaro after closing, the little ones asleep upstairs or on Giulietta's lap. Often her companions would slip into Italian, but Jennifer didn't mind. She was glad not to have to think up things to say. She'd rather sit in silence and lose herself in the picture of Positano on the wall behind the bar—one of five paintings that Paolo had picked up cheaply on the London Road. It was these scenes of the Amalfi coast that had given the restaurant its name, rather than any personal connection to the area. Neither Paolo nor Giulietta had ever been there.

All five paintings were in the same style, made up of lots of tiny little dashes so it looked as though the scenes were quivering, alive. Positano was by far her favourite though, pictured in the evening sun with a peachy sheen across the water. The colourful little houses were stacked up on the cliff, huddled around the crescent cove where fishing boats were hauled up on the sand. Out in the water larger pleasure boats were moored up for the evening, the first few lights shining through the portholes, and on the shore their passengers dined at the restaurants lining the beach. The place was full of people. Not like the people of Stilo but tall, elegant people enjoying themselves. Jennifer could never decide which she'd most like to be: strolling barefoot on the beach, waltzing to the accordion, or standing alone above the town staring out at the sunset.

They had a notice board in the restaurant crammed full of postcards from customers who'd made it; greetings from Amalfi, Positano, Ravello, Sorrento: *It's even more magical in real life! Bellissimo! Sipping Campari and watching the sunset! Tomorrow we catch the boat to Amalfi. Ciao!*

Paolo knew La Mamma was going to be a hit with the customers and he couldn't wait to get her in the kitchen.

"She not happy unless she busy," he said, "and I got plenty to keep her busy. She gonna love it—her grandchildren all fussing around her, her daughters-in-law to boss about, her sons driving her around like she the Queen. She should come here years ago!"

Jennifer and Vito stood at the top of their steps. The sun was high and made a mirror of the car window so that La Mamma, sitting inside, was hidden behind a reflected huddle of hydrangeas. Jennifer had to dip and squint to make out the dark, stern shape of her mother-in-law's profile. She sat immobile, staring straight ahead out of the windscreen, clutching a small duffle bag to her chest as though it were in danger of being snatched. Paolo slammed out of the other side of the car and Giulietta emerged from the back seat. At the same time, Vito set off down the steps so that the three of them arrived together at the passenger door. Paolo opened it, and out poured a sharp torrent of words, like machine gun fire, into the soft English air. The brothers ducked, as though for cover, reaching inside the car and grabbing an elbow each. As soon as La Mamma had been hauled to her feet she turned suddenly and stonily silent.

Jennifer was always shocked by just how small the woman was. Small and compacted like a little lump of volcanic rock. She wore her widow's uniform: a black, long-sleeved, sack-like dress, paled by the sun upon the shoulders as if a coating of dust had settled in the five years since her husband's death. Her steely grey hair was cut short into a prisoner's crop. She'd always had it long, curled into a bun on the back of her head, but Giulietta insisted she lose it for Jennifer's sake, seeing as she'd be the one having to wash it every week. Her face felt the lack of it, seemed ungainly, fearful, like a baby seagull. She stared up at Jennifer and silent gummy tears seeped from the corners of her eyes. Stranded at the top of the steps, Jennifer felt herself on display, as though she were the thing that had been finally reached at the end of the long journey. How very disappointing. She quickly descended the six steps to join the others, bending to kiss La Mamma's damp cheeks. The old woman slipped her arms out of the grip of her two sons and held Jennifer's head in her cold, strong fingers, shaking it slightly and letting out a low moan.

"Mamma!" Vito said sharply, prising his mother's hands off Jennifer's face so that she was free to stand upright again.

"She just so pleased to see you, Jenny," said Paolo. "Look at her! She crying—all of us here together! She just a bit overwhelmed, aren't you Mamma?"

Once they'd manoeuvred her inside, Giulietta showed her to her room, pointing out the little efforts Jennifer had made to make the place feel like home: the flowers, the crochet cloths, the rosewood crucifix above the bed. La Mamma wasn't interested though. She was slow and dazed like a doped elephant newly taken into captivity. Watching her from the door Jennifer pictured her alone in the house on Monday when she and Vito would be at work, shuffling slowly though the empty rooms, spreading her confusion and her misery.

"She speak crazy now," said Giulietta, when La Mamma started to mutter. "It make no more sense to me than it does to you. This rug is no good here." She pointed with her foot at the small rag rug Jennifer had made long ago and at last found a place for. "It's pretty but it's no good, she gonna trip, she gonna break her neck on that."

The following Sunday there was a gathering at the Gambardellis' to celebrate La Mamma's arrival: friends of southern Italian stock who'd been scattered around this southeastern fringe of England like dice flung from the same cup. Over the years they'd found jobs and wives for each other, attended each other's weddings, been godparents to each other's children, and now, bound by all these bloodless ties, had earned a right to be present at every significant event in each other's lives. They were people Jennifer knew from weddings and baptisms but she was not one of them: she and Vito had married late, quietly, and had no children. It was only through Paolo and Giulietta that they clung on, and now La Mamma, who'd given them a reason to play hosts for the first time.

Together, the group was immediately at ease and at home in their house. The adults gathered in the kitchen around the long table Vito had formed from two of Jennifer's dress-cutting trestles, while the children—now sullen, beautiful teenagers—slumped silently in front of the television in the other room. The table was itself divided: the men talking prosciutto and property prices at one end while the women discussed Southend's new shopping centre at the other.

"It's much bigger than the one in Basildon," said Rosa Scura.

"I like the lifts best," said Irene Rossetti.

Giulietta, topping and tailing green beans with Jennifer across the other side of the kitchen, twisted her head round to join in the conversation:

"You shoulda seen Nonna's face when we take her up in one last week," she said. "Anyone would think we was off to the moon!" She contorted her face into a cartoon look of terror and the women at the table threw their heads back in laughter. "When we get to the top I press the button and send us straight back down," said Giulietta, hunching her shoulders and giggling impishly. "Couldn't resist, it was so funny!"

Giulietta had loved The Royals, as the shopping centre had been named: the high glass dome; the pink and green floor tiles; the shiny new shop fronts; the silver escalators smoothly connecting the galleried tiers; the much-talked-about food court where little round tables were bolted to the ground beneath green plastic palm trees. Jennifer had found it hard to summon the same enthusiasm. Wandering among the excited shoppers she'd felt a little sad: this would surely mean the end for Keddies.

"Did you go to the food court, Ma?" said Paola, Giulietta's eldest, who, married now and with a baby, had earned a place among the adults.

"Ah! How beautiful! It's like being on holiday," said Giulietta, who had never been on holiday in her life.

Jennifer felt a sharp rap on the back of her calves and jumped out of the way. It was La Mamma with her stick, who proceeded to flick a green bean dismissively with her finger. Giulietta sighed, put down her knife, and took her firmly by the shoulders. She wouldn't have La Mamma interfering with the cooking. She led her back to the little round stool at the end of the table and pushed her down onto it, telling Paolo to keep her there this time.

"Mamma!" Paolo said grandly, putting an arm round his mother's shoulder and gesturing with the other in a wide sweep around the table. "Look at all your friends come to see you!"

Giulietta had been there all morning helping Jennifer lay on the usual spread. There was lasagne and meatballs, parmigiana and pizza, sausages, green beans, and salad.

The young ones sloped in intermittently to top up their plates to take back in front of the television, while the rest did their best to squeeze in around the table, a constant rearranging of bottles and elbows and half-eaten dishes of food. Jennifer and Giulietta cleared and served, cleared and served, keeping the food coming until eventually they were able to sit down with a slice of cold pizza while the others tucked into their tiramisu.

Exhausted, Jennifer sank into the ebb and flow of after-eating conversation. Her blood and nerves, shaken up from the day's relentless preparations, fizzed in reaction to the atmosphere of sated repose around the dinner table. Her guests sat back in their chairs, offering the warm roundness of their bellies by way of thank you, for she knew by now not to expect any verbal show of gratitude. "What is this 'thank you' all the time?" Vito would say to her. "Don't you ever thank me, Jenny."

Now came coffee, which Vito saw to promptly and proudly—it surprised Jennifer, and made her feel a little guilty too, to see how much he was enjoying tending and talking to these people. He selected the largest of their coffee pots, untwisted the bottom from the top, measured out the water, and then the ground coffee into the correct compartments. Jennifer rose to her feet to fetch their set of pink, gold-rimmed espresso cups from the dresser, a wedding present from Italy. Although their wedding had been a low-key affair, there had been many such gifts: glasses and china, trays, pictures and table linen. Jennifer found them odd and gaudy and cheaply made, but there was space enough in the house to hide them away and slowly they had insinuated themselves into her life so that she no longer questioned their presence: they were simply her things.

The little cups drew admiration as she placed them on the table. Rosa lifted one by the handle and held it up, tilting it to catch the slight iridescence in the pink glaze.

"These are beautiful, Jenny. Look at that, Luisa, see that shimmer?"

These people loved anything small and pretty: coffee cups and serviettes, buttons and bomboniere. With her years in haberdashery, Jennifer knew the comfort of little things too. Over her time there she'd discovered a kind of solace among the tiny pearlised buttons in plastic tubes and the hanging rows of embroidery thread shifting smoothly through the spectrum of colours. In her contented moments she felt as if she were in a museum: cataloguing, displaying, taking care, for reasons more important than mere customers or visitors, who were incidental to some higher and more abstract respect for history or, in this case, haberdashery.

She'd certainly rather be at this end of the table than at the other with La Mamma, who was perched on the outskirts of the men's card game, the tears once more travelling silently down her cheeks.

"What do you think about making a wedding dress, Jenny?" said Luisa Fieri. "You did know Mariangela's engaged?"

Jennifer shifted her chair into a position more congenial to joining in the talk. "Well, I've done plenty of evening gowns and a wedding gown's much the same, there's just a little more of it."

"Can you do a puff sleeve? Mariangela's got her heart set on a puff sleeve, but the prices of the things we've seen so far!"

"Puff sleeves aren't a problem. You send your Mariangela in for a chat."

Luisa folded her arms and smiled. "I will, Jenny, I will. I was thinking, you know that little summer skirt suit you made for me last year? How do you feel about swapping the buttons on the jacket? Mother of pearl maybe. I do think the right buttons make all the difference, don't you?"

This crowd were good and loyal customers of Jennifer's. Even the ones who lived up around Chelmsford and Colchester went out of their way to shop at Enid Scott's rather than the local Marks and Spencer. "Why don't you and Mariangela come in together? We'll get out the pearly buttons and the bridal pattern books and get it all sorted out in one go."

Rosa leaned across the table towards Jennifer. "Bet you can't wait to sort *her* out," she whispered, gesturing with her head towards La Mamma. "Get her out of those rags, get some colour on her. Personally I think it'll do her the world of good. How can she start afresh if she's expected to be in mourning for the rest of her life? It's not natural. And it's not necessary over here either. People start thinking she's dirty, wearing the same thing every day."

"Poor Nonna," sighed Paola. And then, turning to Jennifer, "You want a cuddle, Zia?"

The little bundle was halfway across the table before Jennifer could protest. She preferred to leave babies alone when they were this young. They were not her territory, alien little creatures without control of their limbs, occupying a strange noman's land between the womb and the world. But she took the child—little Francesca—onto her lap, awkwardly cradling her head in the palm of her hand.

"Look at those dear little fingernails!" said Irene, raising one of the baby's tiny fingers. "Why can't they stay this way forever?"

"Soon be bringing boys home, causing trouble," said Giulietta, standing behind Jennifer's chair.

Her sister-in-law had only just finished making babies herself. She'd managed a seamless transition from children to grandchildren, her own youngest, Daniella, only five years older than this little one, whose arrival had continued the constant trickle that was likely to carry on uninterrupted for at least the next twenty-five years, by which time Francesca would no doubt be popping them out herself.

Out they came, these little ones, each of a little less value than the last, their newness dulled by the destiny presented by a string of older cousins and siblings with their mediocre college passes and changing parade of boyfriends and girlfriends. And yet, feeling the warm weightless body in her arms, peering into those strange inward-gazing eyes, Jennifer found herself believing that this one might really be different.

Still, when the doorbell rang Jennifer was glad of an excuse to pass the baby back to Paola. She left the kitchen and walked through to the hall, opening the door to a rush of cold air that made her aware of the accumulated heat in her cheeks as it dissipated into the night.

There was a girl on the doorstep. She stood stiffly with her hands pushed deep into the pockets of a thin red raincoat belted tight around her waist. Her cheeks were rosy with the cold, her face round and plump in a wholesome kind of way, her hair scooped into a pert little ponytail. Jennifer felt she'd seen her before but couldn't place her. She guessed she was a friend of one of Paolo and Giulietta's lot come to rescue them and take them away to a more exciting Sunday evening.

"Hello!" she said in a smart, sprightly voice. Maybe she wasn't from round here after all. "I'm sorry to bother you on a Sunday evening, but I'm looking for a woman called Jennifer Mulholland."

Jennifer was silent, following the small puffs of breath her visitor's words released into the night air.

She laughed a little. "There's no need to look so worried. My name's Lucy Clarkson. I'm from the *Sunday Times* newspaper. I understand a Jennifer Mulholland lives here. Is that you?"

Of course: the little headshot in the newspaper. That's where Jennifer had seen her before. And here she was, a real person, standing on her doorstep.

So she had come for her. Jennifer's initial feeling was of anger. She hadn't foreseen this and she felt intruded upon: how dare she turn up unannounced, interrupting her Sunday evening, asking for a response when all Jennifer felt like doing was curling up in a darkened room. She felt suddenly exhausted. Exhausted but nervy, jazzed up from strong coffee. Worn out from the shopping, the cooking, the making of beds, and all the other small unsuccessful efforts she'd made this past week to ingratiate herself with her mother-in-law. It was simply too much effort to bring herself back to that spacious place she'd felt open up above her head, to call before her that other face—her portrait—which had followed her home like a warm shadow and given her an intimation of a different life. Today was not the day for finding it, or even believing in it. From where she stood in the doorway of her little terrace house it all seemed like some shameful private fantasy that had somehow been found out.

"My name's Mrs. Gambardelli," she said, but she wanted immediately to retract it, throw it off, for it felt like a trap around her ankles.

The girl narrowed her gaze. "Are you sure?"

Jennifer felt flustered now, and mocked. "I should think I know my own name, dear, yes. Now I come to think of it there used to be a Mulholland at this address. I think we used to get letters for a Mulholland, but a long time ago, we haven't had anything for a long time now."

"I see," said Lucy Clarkson. But she continued to stand there and in the silence that followed she kept her eyes on Jennifer, who saw the beginnings of a dimple in her right cheek, and in it the suggestion of a smile. Maybe it was this knowingness, this hint of playfulness, that changed Jennifer's mood. She felt suddenly a little bolder, powerful almost, and couldn't resist:

"What does the *Sunday Times* want with this Mulholland woman anyway? I didn't know she was anything special."

On the train later, when the two of them were speeding towards London in the brightly lit carriage, Lucy had boasted she'd known all along it was her.

The smile appeared fully now, the dimples deep little creases in each cheek. "Well, yes, she is kind of special."

"It's all very mysterious I'm sure."

And now she laughed a little again, leaning in towards the open door. "Have you heard of an artist called Ray Eccles?"

There, she'd said his name. In her well-spoken voice it was a small glinting thing, sitting between them like a diamond in a glass case. Jennifer felt instantly wary again, on her guard.

"I can't say I have but I'm not a follower of art, as I'm sure you can tell." She could hear the baby's disjointed cries from the hot house behind, the cacophony of the television in the front room, the low murmur of voices in the kitchen.

But they sounded distant to her, as if she'd already left them far behind.

Lucy continued:

"He paints these amazing pictures of a woman standing on a beach. Always the same woman standing on the same beach, and yet no one has ever known who she is. But now I do. She's a woman called Jennifer Mulholland. And I was told she lived here at number ten Prittlewell Square. I thought I'd found her... I thought she was you."

Was this Amanda's doing? *This doesn't happen to everyone, Jennifer.* But was she ready for something to happen? Why should Amanda Parsons be the one to decide it should happen now? She felt a certain contrariness rise up within her. But when she spoke again she wished she could be free of it, of her inane words, of her very flesh and bones.

"Well, I hope you find her, dear. I'm sorry I couldn't be more help, it all sounds... yes, fascinating I'm sure. Goodbye now."

And then she closed the door. She froze there for a moment, absorbing its closedness, staring at her hand on the latch, a strange reptilian thing. Then her eyes fell upon the clock on the wall to her left and she must have caught it in transition between one second and the next, for the hand seemed to hang there, paralysed, far longer than it ought, as if giving her a chance to think again. She felt the muscles of her hand clasp around the handle, and then the door was open again. And Lucy Clarkson was still standing there facing her, as if that little interruption in their conversation had never happened.

Ten

Grace lay on the small white sofa at the foot of her bed. She had on an indigo silk robe, something vaguely Japanese she'd once imagined herself wearing about the house in the evening. Its coolness caressed her flesh, the fabric trickling in a low *v* between her small breasts and on down over the top of her right knee, which poked out through the slit. She stretched out her leg, catlike, luxuriating in the spring light pushing softly through the closed orange curtains, and in the fact of lying here at this hour, which was ten in the morning, when children were at school and other people were in offices or buses or taxis.

Ray faced her at the far end of the room, standing on a drift of white dustsheets. He had an easel and a canvas and a small fold-up table by his side arranged with plump tubes of oil paint—no food, this time, she just wanted him to try it. He wore a white smock, one of George's, and looked in every way an artist—or an angel, the way it ballooned out, too big, beneath his sweet, triangular face.

Only an hour ago she'd dropped Mira off at school for the start of the second half of the spring term. They'd walked down through the park and across the front of Buckingham Palace, where they waved good morning to the Queen and carried on down into Belgravia, to the small school for girls where they had concerns about Mira's solitude and her artwork, which showed signs of disturbance. George's impression of Miss Partridge had been the last great hilarity before he fell into his hole.

Grace loved the park in the spring. One morning when you were least expecting it you'd walk down to the lake and—bang, it hit you, those big bursts of colour when all you'd got used to seeing for months were dreary shades of brown and green and grey. You had to be feeling up to it, it was true. Those bright, pert trumpets on their turgid stalks seemed to demand some sort of response. But this year, for once, she'd felt herself stride out to meet them, ready and able.

Once she'd dropped Mira off she walked slowly back through St. James's Park, taking time to taste the crystalline coolness in the air and to watch the trees try and catch the leaves in the very act of forming. She crossed the bridge over the lake, paused out of pure habit to gaze up towards the Admiralty, and then cut across the dew-damp grass onto The Mall. By the time she arrived home she was thoroughly ready to be painted.

She stretched a little again, internally, trying not to move, for at last he had begun. She could feel his eyes on her skin, the very tickle of his brush on her toes as he started work on the extremities. She knew very well the way he painted, the way he started at one corner and worked in. No blocking, no sketching; it was all there from the very beginning, every intricacy complete before he shifted on to a new, clean section of the canvas. She felt her toes keenly, as if they were only now waking up for the very first time: a gradual thaw, a quickening, creeping upwards into her flesh.

She sat for just an hour. It was enough. Her toes had an itch for adventure, and as she dressed, her mind was on a call she'd had yesterday. Giles, a friend of George's, had rung with a lead, a woman by the name of Ruby living on an estate in Hackney whose "memory boxes" he thought would be perfect for the collection. It was George who usually followed these things up, made the initial visit. Sometimes she accompanied him, often she didn't. There was still something about poverty that intimidated her. But her feet had been painted by Ray Eccles today and felt like they could go anywhere. And more than that: she felt herself swelling with some capacity for beauty. George always said that each acquisition to the collection should be a little love story, and she felt, now more than ever, the potential for one to begin.

Feeling adventurous, she went by bus, picking one up on Piccadilly. It was empty enough for her to have the front seat of the top deck all to herself, and she sat there as the bus heaved and swayed over the cars and people below as though it were an elephant she rode. They travelled up through Piccadilly Circus, Shaftesbury Avenue, Charing Cross Road. How gloriously seedy the West End seemed from the damp and smoke-infused upper deck, especially at this hour—midday—when the lights of theatres and advertisements flickered dimly against the weak English sun, and the streets were home to a dazed mix of tourists, tramps, and foreign students eating fast food on the move. They went up through Holborn into Islington and down into Hackney, where Georgian terraces not too dissimilar from the ones lining the streets of Pimlico had boarded-up windows, cracked and blackened brickwork, and weeds sprouting from the gutters. She got off at Dalston Junction, just as Ruby had instructed her over the phone that morning, and turned right down the Kingsland Road.

This was a different country to the one in which she'd boarded the bus: everything coated with a film of dust; a ripe smell of bananas and fried food; shops selling hair and fingernails. She felt momentarily feeble, her body still reeling a little from the movement of the bus. She stood still, steadied herself, then dug her hands deep into the pockets of her long black coat and took off again with long, sure strides until touched once more by the calm and leonine confidence that had got her this far.

She left the Kingsland Road and went over a railway bridge, then she saw the estate she was heading for: huge concrete monoliths towering up into the blank sky like great lumps of regret. When she was among them she saw that they had names: Patience, Dignity, Gladness, Hope. "I live in Hope," Ruby had said.

Grace smiled to herself and followed the sign that pointed her towards Hope, a block located in the centre of the estate, surrounded by cracked paving and patchy grass. Outside, two girls sat tight together on a bench, both with prams and cigarettes and bare legs blotchy from the cold. As she drew closer she felt tender towards them, with their babies and their cold knees.

"Yeah, what you starin' at?" one of them shouted out as Grace approached, and she scurried into the building.

She had been in places like this before, in stairwells that stank of urine and lifts carved with telephone numbers offering her a fuck, but it was no use pretending she felt comfortable in them. How often would she have to ride up and down before she called one of these numbers and said "Okay then, show me a good time"?

Ruby lived on the eleventh floor. Her front door was royal blue and so glossy it could still be wet, or at least sticky, from a new coat of paint. The sallow light that slunk through the dusty window of the stairwell caught the ghosts of past carvings beneath the surface. *Fat Tramp.*

Grace pressed her finger to the greasy bell and heard it rattle away inside. It was some time before it was answered— by a woman as wide as the doorway, in a skirt that hung round her middle like a curtain round a cubicle in a cheap clothing store. Oh dear. Grace had trouble with fatness. She found it hard to forgive, somehow. It showed such a terrible lack of self-control.

"You must be Ruby," she said.

"Are you the one what's come to buy my boxes?"

"Well—" Grace laughed. So presumptuous! "I'd love to see them… if you'd let me?"

The woman turned her back and started down the hallway, disappearing into the far room to the left. How dismal, thought Grace, to be able to stand here in the open doorway and to see in one short glance the entire layout of the apartment, the end of it just a few metres in front of her at the dead end of the little passage, and four narrow doors opening uniformly off it all that was offered by way of diversion. She stepped forward and closed the door behind her, following Ruby into the second room on the left, a small cube of a living room upon which the ceiling bore down in vicious Artex spikes tipped with resinous deposits of nicotine, like stalactites starting to form.

Grace drifted unthinkingly towards the window and the view. She'd always harboured the suspicion that tower blocks like this, much taller than her own, would be the most wonderful places to live: high and free above the city.

But now she'd found her way into one and was looking from the window, mired on the outside with a lunar-like sediment, she concluded that one could be *too* high, there could be too *much* sky, that from up here the city seemed just a low and dreary sprawl.

"What a wonderful view!" she said.

"Man two floors up threw 'imself out last week," said Ruby, from behind her.

"Oh, how dreadful!" Grace felt suddenly faint—for the first time in her life she actually felt as if she might faint. She backed away from the window and slunk into a chair as calmly as she could manage. The thought of fainting had always rather thrilled her, but to do it for the first time here would be terrible: to wake up with Ruby bearing down on her... breathing on her... I must try and love this woman, she thought, remembering why she was here.

Her head began to clear and she looked with studied brightness around the room. There was barely a thing in it. She and Ruby sat opposite each other on the only two chairs—armchairs that looked overweight themselves, with great rolls of peachy fat. Clearly they'd started life as an identical pair but the one Ruby sat in was showing the strain of being preferred, the velvety fabric worn bare over the arms and headrest, the buckled frame visible beneath the frayed hem of Ruby's skirt. Between them was a small oval coffee table, and that completed the furniture. There were no pictures on the walls, no curtains; just one bare, lit bulb hanging from the ceiling. But round the edges of the room, following the line of the skirting and barely noticeable at first, was a neat line of tiny, whitish boxes. "Is that them?" Grace asked, nodding towards the floor.

"Memory boxes," said Ruby.

"Can I have a look?"

Ruby pointed, quite specifically, to a section of skirting to the right of the doorframe. "Over there," she said, and Grace rose slowly from her chair, making her way cautiously towards the door.

"Here?" said Grace, pointing down in front of her feet.

"Fine," said Ruby.

Grace crouched, and then bent her head further towards the floor, for the boxes seemed somehow out of focus, blurred. She couldn't work out what it was, and then she saw: each was covered with a thick layer of wax. Beneath were faces, photographs—couples, family groupings, small children holding hands—cut out and stuck together in a kind of collage. Their eyes strained up towards her, and hers strained down towards them as though they were staring at each other across the veil of time, trying to make each other out. In the small spaces between the pictures, she could see indistinct lines of printed typeface, showing that Ruby had made the boxes from newspaper. The words, again, seemed out of focus, as though they would gather and sharpen into meaning if she could only find the right distance to read them from. But always they remained just the other side of clarity.

She peered closer, on all fours now, and touched one. It sprung slightly under her finger; they were light, these boxes, borne aloft by the deep pile of the carpet. Her nose caught dampness in the fibres, and she could see little drops of wax now, everywhere, clinging to the synthetic twists like early morning dew. Dirt and ash was caught up in them too—and life, she felt certain, must be going on in there, tiny births and deaths. She picked up a box and placed it on her palm. It fitted neatly into her hand. The underneath was the only side not coated with wax, just the thin, bare newspaper, and she could feel the small and separate weights of the things inside.

She stood up and walked back over to Ruby, lowering her palm to offer her the box. Ruby picked it up between forefinger and thumb and held it up, looking up at the underside. "Fifth September, '85," she said, reading off what was written there. "This one's fine. I wait a year, see, before I open 'em up. That way I've forgotten what I put inside and it's a nice surprise. I was gonna open one this morning but I waited for you, see."

Ruby put the box down in the middle of the table, spreading her knees wide and leaning forward into the gap they created. There was an eagerness in the gesture, like sleeves being rolled up, and something warm, too, in the fact of having been waited for. Grace knelt down at the end of the table, a little excited, feeling for the first time that she wanted to be close to this woman. There was a slight agitation too in the stagnant air, as if the strange little box was a pebble that had plopped into the room and caused ripples to spread out towards the walls.

Ruby lifted off the lid, a flat thing, about a centimetre thick with wax. "Hello my treasures," she whispered, and then lifted her head towards Grace, her greasy hair falling down over her eyes. She smiled. Then she looked back down into the box and, very slowly, one by one, pulled out the contents, holding each thing up to the weak light with the same care and admiration with which Christopher Earnest had held the silk tie to catch the glint of the chandelier. A cigarette butt; a silver ring-pull; a dry, brown leaf; a crumpled till receipt; a one-penny piece; and a discarded baby's pacifier. This last thing she held up longer than the others, the plastic handle pinched between her fingertips, the rubber teat pointing to the ceiling. "They come from the angels, these," she said, twisting it slowly one way and then the other. It was a horrid thing, the pallid pink plastic scuffed around the edges, the rubber as thick and yellow as dead skin. But as Grace looked at it she started to see there was something peculiarly puzzling about it, something intimate and alien. She glanced then at Ruby's face, held in profile. Her gaze was concentrated upwards, her mouth slightly open, and Grace suddenly saw quite startlingly that she'd once been a child, that this huge, lumpish, lank-haired creature had once been a dear little girl.

Ruby lowered the pacifier back into the box along with the rest of the things and put the lid back on carefully. She sat up and looked at Grace.

"I love it," said Grace quietly, looking up at her.

"They ain't cheap, mind," said Ruby. "I won't sell for less than two hundred pound a box."

Grace returned in a taxi, and beside her on the back seat sat an old shoebox Ruby had given her filled with five of her memory boxes. She felt them beside her like something small and alive, a hamster perhaps. She smiled—a hamster!—pleased with the analogy, for it so perfectly described the small thrill of new responsibility and companionship that had come with her purchase, the sort of pleasure that accompanies the taking home of a new pet rather than, say, a new baby which was too... too *much*, somehow, to be pleasurable.

Of course what lay beside her was much better than a silly hamster. It was Art. And the wonderful thing was that she had made it so. She thought of her cheque for one thousand pounds lying on the small, chipped coffee table. How marvellously it had transformed in her mind the room she had left behind, which existed now, as she trundled up towards Angel, as a place of heartbreaking beauty. She pictured Ruby—gloriously fat—seated stately in her collapsing armchair, the walls of the empty room pressing yellowly upon her, the man two floors up sailing past the window like a dying bird, and the name of the block—"Hope"—throbbing somewhere in the sky above, a faded neon sign.

She was already thinking of an exhibition, in the Serpentine perhaps: all of Ruby's memory boxes arranged open on the floor in neat rows, the precise, uniform spaces between them bristling and fizzing with an inexplicable energy.

At home she went straight in to George, curled in his bed like a crab under a rock.

"I bought something," she announced, sitting down on the edge of the bed with the shoebox on her lap. George's gaze bored blank into her thigh. "Dear George," she said, and bent to kiss him, prompt and efficient, on the side of his head. Surely he could at least *try* to feel better.

She removed herself and the shoebox from the bed and knelt on the floor, her face close and level with his. "I've been to the dreariest block of flats you can imagine!" she whispered with determined eagerness. "You should be proud of me, it was beautifully grim." She reached into the shoebox beside her and, with both hands, lifted out one of the memory boxes, placing it on the bed right in front of him to force his eyes into activity: to focus or close. "They're made by a woman called Ruby. I loved her. I completely fell in love with her!" She watched his eyes reel from the proximity and she laughed, shifting the box a little further away. His eyes narrowed, striving to see the clusters of faded faces beneath the opacity of the wax. Slowly, he reached a pale finger out from under the duvet to touch it. His brow tensed a little, gathering strength, and Grace watched optimistically for the first signs of recovery, which often showed here as a straining for movement in the skull. He prodded at the box and it was just enough to topple it off the edge of the bed onto the floor, spilling its contents, like a tiny rubbish bin, across the carpet.

So much for the upward tilt. Grace did not try again. Instead she found fewer and fewer reasons to enter the dark little room at the back of the apartment. Something new was happening outside it and for once she felt behind it, effective and capable. In the mornings, after dropping Mira off at school, she sat for Ray, a most delicious start to the day. Stretched out on the white sofa, naked beneath her indigo robe, she felt the movement of his attention as it shifted slowly up her body like a rising tide, the tingle creeping from her toes, up behind her knees, between her thighs. She felt herself being filled in, fashioned anew, a second, truer skin knitting itself around her like a healing wound. By the end of the hour her body ached with its own fullness, as if she might burst open were he to touch her.

The afternoons she spent out visiting and buying, looking daily for new little love stories to begin. George had neglected things and his study was full of scribbled notes: names and addresses of potential new artists, trails abandoned when he stumbled into his hole.

> Valerie. Knitter. Lewisham. 23 Dover Road. No phone. Sweet person. Careful—very prudish!
> FANTASTIC MASKS.

Grace took up these scraps, the slant and disorder of the handwriting encouraging a sense of urgency, as if the treasure were in danger of being discovered by someone else. She went to Lewisham to see Valerie and her knitted masks, to Brixton to see Victor and his budgerigars made of crushed glass, and to Chelsea to listen to an old major's dreams of pursuing a young woman through a forest. At the end of the dream she always turned round and he saw she had the face of a eagle, a vision he'd painted over and over on small wooden tablets that he hung from the ceiling of his antiques-filled sitting room, so low that Grace had to weave between them as she crossed the room to greet him.

Eleven

All this time, Grace had resisted looking at the painting. It had been standing in her bedroom for three weeks, uncovered, and not once had she walked round the other side to take a look. As the days went on it asserted its presence more and more. The solid rectangle of canvas and the wide stance of the easel grew into a kind of sentinel, standing guard over the secret that lay on the other side. What was it? Who was waiting behind there? The more she wanted to know the less she dared to look. Until one evening. She was alone downstairs, as she often was after Mira had gone to bed. She'd been writing a proposal for the exhibition she had in mind at the Serpentine but had put down her pen and moved over to the sofa, where she sat listening to the music she'd had playing in the background. She turned up the volume. The male voice on the cassette was soft and melancholy, but behind it was a beat, crazy and strong, that made her feel strangely exhilarated. Facing the large window that overlooked the park, she stared at her own reflection amidst the treetops and felt as though she were gearing up for something, about to launch off and set sail on her sofa out across the park and over the rooftops of Kensington. She clutched her own hand, as though in readiness, but the thrust of the moment took her not out of the window but upstairs to her bedroom, feeling bold and excited and surer than ever of the beauty of what she would find.

She stood behind the canvas and rested her hand upon the top edge, lightly as though on the shoulder of a lover. And then she circled slowly around to face it. Herself, as she really was.

It took less than a heartbeat for Grace to realize that she was not looking at herself at all, for the image that faced her was so horribly familiar. The beach, the woman, a gaze that stared disinterestedly through her. She'd sat in front of him for three weeks and he hadn't seen her. How odd to discover one didn't exist.

The paint was still wet. She reached out a finger to touch it, leaving a small, smeared impression just below an eye. She thought of George next door in his hole. What a warm, comfortable place it must be. All this time she'd felt herself on the ascent: collecting, sitting for Ray, the days stacking up on top of one another like they were really adding up to something. The gleaming silk tie, Ruby in her concrete tower, the art she'd added to the collection. And behind it all, the thing that propped it all up, this painting.

How quickly it all drained away, and how weak and hollow she felt now, as if even her insides had deserted her.

She walked out of the room onto the landing. She didn't know what to do or where to put herself. It wasn't late but everyone else was in bed: Mira, a child; George, who never came out of it; and Ray... She stood still in front of the door to his room feeling detached from herself, watching for what she might do next. Her hand rested lightly on the door handle, lowered it, the door opening slowly and quietly. Her steps sounded softly on the bare floor as she crossed the room to the bed.

He slept with his face to the ceiling, open and unguarded. Like a tiny moon it seemed to gather what little light there was in the room, while the walls lurked thick with shadows and painted faces. An imaginary woman who was more real than *she* was. She stood over him. Trespassing in his dreams. And then she hit him. It was a pathetic, hesitant slap, landing clumsily on the side of his forehead, barely forceful enough to wake him. She hit him again. More forceful this time. Her fist in his eye. It opened. Between her blows he did open his eyes and he looked straight at her. Fear and confusion. But he didn't attempt to escape her or even to defend himself. And she didn't feel like an attacker. Her movements were too slow and too silent for that. She felt the growing sting in her knuckles, but inside she was empty, just watching his face transform, soft and pliable like a slab of clay. First the colour bloomed around his eye. Then it emerged from his nostril, making its way slowly across his cheek and spreading over the white pillow.

There must have been some noise. Perhaps there was a lot, because George appeared in the doorway. The moment she saw him she stopped. Gentle George, who would never hurt anyone. She saw then what she had done.

"Oh, Grace," he said quietly. Then he said it again, "Oh, Grace", as he walked over and stood behind her, taking hold of her trembling arm. He held her forearm firmly, though not in restraint, for she was clearly finished. She began to shake all over and he held her with both hands now, one on each arm, as they looked down at the poor beaten creature in his bed, curled on his side with his knees tucked into his chest.

George let her go and dropped to his knees, putting a hand to Ray's head. He turned and looked up at her. "You go, I'll deal with this," he said firmly.

She didn't question his presence, the calm competence with which he who had been incapable of leaving his bed for weeks now began to tend to Ray. She did as she was told.

As she walked down the hallway to her room, the bell rang. It was craziness to answer it but she had no thoughts right now. Robotic, she simply went where she was called. She walked past her bedroom and through to the entry phone by the front door. "Hello?"

"Mrs. Zoob?"

"Yes."

"This is Lucy Clarkson. From the *Sunday Times*? I wondered if I could come up and talk to you a moment."

"But it's so late," Grace said, looking at her watch and seeing that it was not as late as it seemed.

"I know, I'm sorry, but would you mind?"

Grace looked at the button that, when pressed, would open the door into the lobby. It jittered like a dying fly on the wall.

"Well, you're here now."

In fact she felt suddenly very much in need of this sort of company. It was as though life, instead of punishing her, had taken pity and, seeing just what she needed, had delivered a young journalist to her door. Someone with whom she could be Grace Zoob, art collector, again. "We're on the top floor," she said, and held her finger firmly down on the button.

The girl's face, when it arrived outside the apartment, had the flush of the night on it, shining like a hard little apple. Round and round and round it went without directing you anywhere in particular. There was someone with her, the sudden awareness of which interrupted Grace's attempts at a smile. "I wasn't expecting two of you," she said.

"No," said the girl, turning to beam at the woman standing by her side who, distinctly awkward in a shapeless brown woollen coat, hardly seemed worthy of eliciting such excitement. "I didn't want to explain over the intercom but... can we come in?'

"Sure," said Grace, standing aside to let them pass and leading them through to the sitting room.

She switched on a lamp and, walking across the room towards another, said, "I hope you're not going to ask me to see the new Eccles work for the exhibition because I shan't show you."

Lucy laughed. "No, I wouldn't dream of it!" She walked over to the window and leaned towards the glass, peering out. "Isn't it a beautiful evening? We walked right across the park to get here and the moonlight was all draped across the grass."

"It's the streetlamps," said Grace. "We have no concept of moonlight in London."

She turned quickly round towards the other, older woman who was hovering moth-like beside the standing lamp, her brown woollen coat still firmly buttoned up.

"I'm sorry, I must introduce you," said Lucy. She raised her arm towards her companion. "This is Jennifer Mulholland. I've brought her here from Southend-on-Sea."

Still that ridiculous smile, as if something marvellous should be understood from this.

"She's the one in Ray's paintings!"

Dear God, not this. Not this now.

"Really?" said Grace slowly. "The *One*?"

Again, that short laugh. Grace disliked people who were always laughing for no reason. "Yes. Can you believe it? I had a call from someone who knew her once. It's a strange story. Quite beautiful." More laughter. "I'm sorry, you must know it already. But isn't it exciting that we've found her? I thought I should bring her to meet you at once."

"And how did you expect me to react?"

Grace needed some help because this was not what she had opened the door to.

"I suppose I thought you'd be excited too. I guess you know that Jennifer and Ray have never actually met?"

"Well, perhaps you'd like to meet him now?" said Grace, gesturing towards the door. "He doesn't look too pretty, I've just beaten him up. You see, I wanted him to paint me. I wanted him to paint me and I sat there practically naked in front of him for three weeks believing that he *was* painting me and all he painted was you! Tell me, what does it feel like to be so… so inspiring?"

Her words had made the woman blush. She'd stepped out from under the light and was standing now behind the armchair. "Well, I, I really wouldn't know, I didn't—"

"I'm sorry," Lucy cut in. "We really didn't mean to disrupt anything. You're all very happy here, I know. Ray's Mira's father and—"

Grace laughed. It seemed too ridiculous. "Ray's not Mira's father! You think anyone could get close to him except… your *friend* here?" She looked away towards the room's strip of window. In reflection she watched Lucy join Jennifer protectively behind the armchair. She turned to face them. "Who are you anyway? I mean… what do you *do*?"

The woman hesitated, and then spoke. Her voice was small and dry. "I run a small ladies' dress shop in Westcliff-on-Sea."

Grace sat down on the sofa. She felt suddenly exhausted. A small ladies' dress shop in Westcliff-on-Sea. Nothing made any sense to her. It *had* made sense to her once. Until only an hour ago, it had all made sense. It had been bizarre and beautiful and she had been part of it. A man possessed by beauty. A man who couldn't stop painting. They had found him and they had taken him home. And his paintings, his silent mysterious energy, had filled their home. But that the face should be a real face. That it should be *this* face. This soft, mothy face. That the woman on the beach should be here, now, in her apartment, wearing a brown woollen coat. That she should run a small ladies' dress shop in Westcliff-on-Sea. That didn't make any sense. She was never part of the story.

"I think it would make a really interesting story for the paper," said Lucy suddenly.

"Oh, I'm sure it would," said Grace, snapping out of her fatigue. "What would it be? A photograph of Miss—I'm sorry, what was it? Macdonald?—on Southend beach next to a picture of one of Ray's paintings? A kind of spot-the-difference? Or perhaps the two of them together, reunited at last. Really, I'm sorry to break it to you, my dear, but if Ray wanted to find you do you not think he would have done so already? What you don't seem to understand is that this is not real life. This is art. Maybe he saw you once. God knows why but you seem to have stuck in his mind. But don't you *see*? It's not *you* in those paintings. This goes *way* beyond you. *You* don't matter at all."

"I don't agree," said Lucy, "I think people would be fascinated."

"Of course you do. You just care about your little story which is going to get your little name in the newspaper and allow you to keep your little job for a little while longer. I'll tell you what would make a better story. I'm not joking. I just beat the shit out of him. You could probably get me arrested. In fact, why don't you? Why don't you just call the police? You can use my phone. You know, I think I'm going crazy. I could quite easily hit you, too, in a minute. God knows I'm sick of the sight of you. I mean, I can actually see it now. It really is you in his paintings, isn't it? Of course, you've spoiled them for me now. Your fat face has completely—"

"Hang on there," Lucy cut in. "I think we should probably leave." She took Jennifer's arm and made hurriedly towards the door. "I'm sorry to have interrupted your evening."

And then all of a sudden they'd left the room. There were so many clocks in that room, all ticking out of sync. Grace heard amongst them the louder click of the door closing and knew they had left.

She stood alone in the lamplight. As the silence ticked around her all the things in the room—the lamps, the furniture, the paintings on the walls, the beautiful and thoughtfully placed objects—took a cool step back. It came upon her now: a terrible and pressing remorse. Ray. She had hurt him. She had crushed her butterfly. And that woman in her brown woollen coat was buzzing restlessly around her mind, for she didn't know what to do with the thought or the knowledge of her. She listened for noises coming from the back of the apartment but there were none. Eventually she walked slowly down the passageway and stopped outside Ray's door. Her hand wobbled on the door handle as she entered. Now she would have to face George. She both needed and feared him.

But the room was empty. The bed was empty. She stood beside it. The cover had been pushed aside to reveal the crumpled sheet. A blossom of blood on the pillow. She reached down and touched it dreamily with her finger and then, her heart waking up, turned quickly. Suddenly panicked she rushed through to George's room.

"He's gone!" she said, throwing back the door, her voice shrill and breaking.

"It's ok, Grace." George was sitting at his desk. His face was calm and forgiving. What was this? He'd chosen *now* to come out of it? To climb out of his hole? For weeks he'd been there, washed up, wretched. And then all of a sudden as if it had never happened. How dare he!

"Where is he?" she demanded.

"He's fine, Grace. I cleaned him up. He just said he needed to get some air."

"I didn't see him go."

"Who've you been talking to? Who came?"

"You let him *go*?"

George laughed. He took her hand and pulled her to him. "Gracie! Come on. Everything's going to be okay. It really wasn't as bad as it seemed, just give him some space now. We can recover from this."

"I need to find him," she said, resisting his touch, invasive as it curled around her buttock. She turned and walked quickly from the room.

He called after her: "Let's go away for a while, a holiday!"

She left the front door open behind her and ran down the steps to the lobby, her socks slipping on the cool stone. She heaved open the glass door and stood outside in the cold, looking up and down the narrow street. There was nobody. He would have cut through into the park. Standing at the end of the passage that led beneath the apartment block she saw two figures framed by and blocking the end of the dark tunnel. She knew them instantly as the woman in the brown woollen coat and the girl, who stood facing the older woman with a hand on her arm. She couldn't pass them. She was trapped. The cold and the damp pushed up through her socks as she stood impatiently waiting for them to move on, but they remained. She would go up again and look from the window; maybe she would have a better chance of seeing him from there anyway.

But she saw nothing. Just a couple walking close against the cold as they cut across to the Tube. She knew he had gone. The early blossom on the low trees, stripped of its pink by the night, appeared dull and flabby, like clusters of frogspawn. A gross eruption of life that smothered the truth: that all came to nothing in the end.

*

They did go on holiday. They went to the cottage in Norfolk. By that time they had given up hope of Ray returning. Unfathomably, George was jubilant. He seemed to see it as a fresh start. At least it had appeared that way.

She should have seen what was coming but she didn't, not at all. He had that raw and crazy energy back that she'd once loved, and she tried to again, to let her sadness be consumed within it. But it was different: more reckless, dangerous, and he wasn't taking her with him this time.

He was hungry for her though, and she wanted him, too; she wanted to be buried in sensation. They had more sex than they'd had in years. As soon as Mira was asleep in her little attic bedroom he was on Grace, taking her clothes off in front of the fire where their bodies would twist and turn for hours like wrestlers, his wide wet mouth consuming her as if he was trying to get through her to something else beyond.

Afterwards, her memories of that holiday were so vivid they threatened to erase all the rest, the many years of their togetherness. She resented that. It was selfish of him to leave her with such a painful series of compositions. She saw them like pictures on a wall. Three bodies arranged in the bleak landscape, or in the small, low-ceilinged rooms of the cottage, close to one another. Mira curled in George's lap like a cat in the lamplight. Naked limbs entwined before the fire. Three lone figures strung out across the wide and empty beach. Together hand in hand with the child between them, blown on by the crazy wind. Mira turning cartwheels on the hard, wet sand. And then the last one: George striding out, naked and fearless, into the icy endless sea. She shouted to him. She wanted him to turn and wave but he didn't. She watched him go deeper. She watched his dark head popping up like a seal among the small choppy waves. And then she couldn't see him any more.

Twelve

Ray was sitting on a bench in Green Park with a pigeon on his lap; Grace might easily have spotted him, had not panic and guilt clouded her eyes.

The bird had caught his attention as he'd approached the bench because it hadn't flown away as he drew near. Even when he sat down it had stayed there, right beside his foot. It moved only a little, turning in a small uncertain circle. It was then, as its head came briefly into the soft light of a nearby lamp, that he noticed its eye was hurt.

"You poor thing," he whispered, his own eye throbbing in sympathy. He reached down and tentatively stroked its feathered back with the tips of his fingers. He had never touched a bird before. It didn't flinch, so he ran his palm lightly along the length of it. And still it didn't try to move away. In fact it seemed glad of the contact, pressing its body into his hand to meet his touch. It was this reaction that prompted him to try picking it up. He bent down and cupped his hands gently around its breast and, meeting no resistance, brought it up to his lap. Its claws scrabbled for a moment on the thin, smooth cotton of his pyjama trousers and then tucked in neatly under its body as it settled down. He kept his hands cupped around the bird, feeling the small skeleton beneath the soft feathers, and beneath that the quick beat of its tiny heart.

There he sat with the pigeon on his lap. If he had looked up he would have seen the flat in which he had spent the last ten years of his life, just a short distance across the park and the only one in the building with a light on in the front room. Despite the many years ahead in which he would wander this city, he would never return there, or even to this park. In fact, his memories of the place would be almost entirely limited to those that filled his head at this very moment, clear not only because they were of events that had only just occurred but because they were arriving in a mind almost entirely free of other memories.

For many years now there simply hadn't been room for them, for anything other than what had been placed before his eyes in that moment in which he'd knelt upon the shingle at East Beach, Shoeburyness, on the 12th of June 1976. Less than a moment: a moment between moments. Stuck in the passage between one heartbeat and the next he had seen and remembered everything. If you cannot forget, you cannot move on. It had filled him up entirely. But now he had been struck on the head again. Not by a bird falling from the sky but by Grace Zoob. And what had filled him was emptying away. He felt it physically, like something draining from his body; even the awareness of it being something worth keeping hold of was already lost to him forever. And there in the empty chamber it left behind remained only the events of the past hour, in which he had woken to see Grace Zoob's face looming over him and had felt her fist smack into his eye and the sting it left behind and had known instantly that he needed to leave that place. On his way out he had automatically taken his jacket from where it hung beside the front door and as he walked though the dark passage beneath the apartment building he'd slipped it on, reaching his hand into the pocket where he felt the silky threads of a tie that was rolled up inside. He'd held onto it tightly, for the draining sensation had already begun and was making him feel faint. Perhaps it was this that had caused him to head for the first bench he saw and to focus his dizzy mind upon this poor pigeon.

In time the pigeon's eye would heal and no longer give her pain, although it was clear she'd lost the sight in it. The other eye saw clearly enough, but having only one affected her balance and prevented her from flying. She didn't even seem interested in trying, despite Ray's encouragement. But even if she had been able, the pigeon wouldn't have gone far. From the plaintive look with which her good eye fixed him on that bench in Green Park, Ray understood that the pigeon both wanted and needed to be near him. And maybe the pigeon understood that Ray needed the same from her. As time went on, that look would develop into one of affection, even love.

Pigeon would teach Ray a lot about living on the streets. She would teach him how to scavenge for food, how to take what he could find and the places where people left it out. She would teach him the best places to hide away and bed down for the night, and how to keep warm and safe, burying his head in the crook of his arm, his jacket wrapped wing-like around him. She would teach him to take what he needed from people but otherwise to stay out of their way. They didn't need company. Pigeon shied away from the other pigeons as much as Ray did from other people, and Ray felt the need to protect her from those other birds with their proud chests and their small sharp beaks, which he suspected were the cause of his friend's injury. If ever they came across a large flock he would lift her up and tuck her away in his pocket, stroking his thumb over the little round head and tattered wings, muttering to her in the coos and soft throaty warbles that would come to take over from words.

Thirteen

Ten years after George Zoob walked into the sea at Brancaster Beach, Mira Zoob was an orphan. Although not technically, for her mother died on the day of her eighteenth birthday. She couldn't remember exactly when cancer had been diagnosed but it couldn't have been long after George's death, for Mira struggled to recall a time when it hadn't been there. Fighting it replaced art collecting as her mother's occupation, although she wasn't much good at it. They moved out of London to a cottage in Oxfordshire and Mira went to a school for girls who wore green blazers and grey felt hats. She made a career out of shocking her teachers and classmates, which wasn't hard. Bored by the usual transgressions, she started a witches' coven, performing skyclad rituals in the woods and teaching her Pony Club friends to kiss with tongues. She soon tired of that too, though. Leaving it to her now-devoted protégées she became studious and solitary. She walked for hours alone beside the little river that meandered through the fields below the cottage. Sometimes her mother joined her, but the two of them were no longer close. Grace was too busy with the cancer, that demanding but never-mentioned guest in their house. She attacked it mostly with books on new nutritional theories, which lay half-read all over the cottage, and culinary equipment: juicers and sprouters and blenders. There were treatments at hospitals. Poisons injected into her body which she railed against but submitted herself to all the same. Before Mira was considered old enough to look after herself, she would be taken to the elderly couple next door while these treatments were taking place and taking their toll. They would give her mugs of milky tea and try and put her to bed in the middle of the afternoon.

Although she had a stubborn determination to beat the disease, her mother had no real desire to live, a truth that reached Mira only as an underlying atmosphere in the house, persuading her to find ways to be out of it as much as possible. The cottage was cluttered and dusty, the air stale. No amount of sprouted mung beans could fix the damage done by grief and sadness and loss of hope.

Eventually they moved back to London, where Grace thought she would be in more competent hands. Back to the apartment overlooking Green Park, stripped now of all its artwork. Mira had only vague memories of the place, most of them based on the pictures—monsters and faces and strange abstract shapes that her childish imagination had invested with animal or human forms— and her father, George, who sang to her sometimes at night and nuzzled his big nose into her eye sockets. None of them were triggered by this empty white box in which she found herself spending more and more time alone. Her mother was more often than not at the hospital and, at seventeen, she was now old enough to look after herself. Eventually it was clear that her mother wasn't coming home.

Sometimes Gregoire du Feu, who was painting a portrait of the dying Grace in her hospital bed, would come back to the apartment with her. He was a bastard, her mother was right, but she liked the way his smoke filled the apartment and that he didn't treat her as a child, showing no respect for her age or the usual rules of discretion. They would return from the hospital in a taxi together and sit in front of the large bare windows overlooking the park, just smoking and drinking whisky.

"You know I always rather fancied your mother. Never fucked her, though. Never tried. I think she wanted me to though. I think she wanted me to at least try. And fail of course." He laughed.

"What about my father?"

"George? Oh, beautiful George. What a cowardly bastard, leaving the two of you."

They sucked on their cigarettes and Mira tried to copy the way he exhaled, drawing his lower lip up to send the smoke above his head.

"You were such a beautiful child," he said, crossing his legs. They were facing each other in two black leather chairs, their whisky glasses on the small round table between them. "I fantasized about you. I fantasized about getting into your little panties. Does that make me a bad man?"

Two weeks later, Grace nearing the end, Mira lost her virginity to him. She knew it shouldn't have happened but it did and it carried on happening. For a while they were lovers. There was only the sex, the cigarette, and the glass of whisky. Nothing else. He didn't try to be tender or pretend to be in love with her, which she appreciated. She couldn't have coped with that. When he touched her, her body responded in a way that terrified her at first. She didn't know it could do that, that she was capable of that level of sensation. All her nerves spiralling down to a little ball of fire, as if she was the centre of the world. That her memories of her mother's funeral should be tied up with the taste of Gregoire du Feu's cock was something she later profoundly regretted, but at the time it had seemed not just to make sense but to be necessary.

It was only in the last days, made dazed and senseless by morphine, that her mother started to talk about Ray Eccles. Barely conscious, she would call out his name. Other times she might look at Mira, direct and urgent:

"Where's Ray?"

"Bring Ray, Mira, I want to see him."

"You will look after Ray, won't you?"

Mira knew the name, she knew he had been someone important to her mother and father and that he had lived with them for a time, but she barely remembered him beyond a vague presence: kindly, benign, out of bounds. She didn't act on her mother's requests. What could she do? Many things were said, and much of it made little or no sense, plus there wasn't time now. But afterwards, quite a long time afterwards, months after she'd freed herself from Gregoire du Feu, she came across a newspaper cutting while sorting through her mother's things. It was a task she attacked sporadically and listlessly. Whole days could be consumed by a box of cuttings like this: reading one, setting it aside, lying back and staring at the ceiling for a while, hours maybe; reading another; unfolding the brittle pages; folding them up again; eventually getting to the end without any clearer idea of what to do with them; putting them all back in the box; noticing that it had got dark outside. But this particular cutting was different.

*Both men apparently remain ignorant (as does
Grace) as to which of them is the biological
father. "We all love, care for, and look after
Mira. It doesn't help to start labelling people—
this man is your father, this man is not. I don't
know myself and I don't care."*

Well, she did. She cared. Maybe she wasn't completely
alone in the world after all.

It freaked people out that she had no parents. Her fellow
students at Central Staint Martins, where Gregoire du Feu
had persuaded her to enrol on a course, couldn't imagine that
much loss. They didn't want to, either, and avoided getting
too close. She was popular though, for she was beautiful
and rich and had connections in the art world, as well as
her own flat overlooking Green Park. She took to throwing
parties, or allowing them to happen, and it would be two or
three days before the last slow and stupefied stragglers left.
She liked them, her peers, the way their bodies filled up her
flat, but she didn't know them and she didn't care to. She
had nothing in common with them. She didn't drink beer
or do drugs or fuck anyone her own age. There had been
others after Gregoire, mostly friends of George and Grace's,
other collectors or owners of small commercial galleries,
men who felt a vague responsibility for her but couldn't
help themselves. They weren't like Gregoire though. They
touched her body with trepidation as if worried it might
break, and afterwards expressed fatherly concern. "You
should sell this place. Too many memories. I could help
you, it's worth a lot of money you know."

Tom was her attempt to kick the habit. He was a boy in her
year who had stayed on after a party. She'd been sitting in the

kitchen when he'd come in and offered to make her a coffee. She'd assented absent-mindedly, but when he presented it to her on the kitchen table it was a thing of such beauty that she looked at him properly for the first time, noticing his pale green eyes and the neat little dimple in his chin. He'd found one of Grace's special powder-blue coffee cups that Mira had forgotten existed. The coffee was fresh and black, little creamy islands still whirling and settling on the surface from the pour. She had no idea where he'd got it from, as her own cupboards were practically bare. On the saucer was a small, shiny spoon, and by the side a little white jug filled with warm milk. No one had ever given her anything so lovely. She determined to try and fall in love with this boy.

"Do you want to come with me to Southend today? I have a house there."

He wanted to know her. On the train he sat opposite her, leaning forward, his elbows resting on his knees. The scenery was flat and unremarkable until they reached the edges of the estuary, where the mudflats, cleaved by tiny rivulets and made gleaming and voluptuous by the sun, had a sensual beauty.

"My father grew up here."

"Someone told me your parents—"

"Were dead?"

"Yes."

"My mother died on my eighteenth birthday. But my father's still alive, I just haven't seen him in a while. He left when I was little."

"Mine too."

"He's an artist. An Outsider Artist. Do you know what that means?"

Tom said he did, but she told him anyway.

"They're artists who don't see themselves as artists. Untrained and urged to create by something other than a desire to exhibit or achieve recognition. Often they're loonies, but my dad isn't. He was just an ordinary guy, worked in an office, and then for some reason became obsessed with this woman he saw on the beach."

"Your mother?"

"No. But my mother discovered him. He came to live with her in London, at my flat. I was born not long after. It was his, the house we're visiting."

She didn't tell him anything else. He must have been expecting a normal house. Mira had no real idea herself what she might find. Her mother had been terribly disorganized but Mira had managed to uncover a set of keys with a label on: No. 8. It had to be them.

They left the train at Shoeburyness and got a taxi from the station. The roads were empty, the sky too. Not a cloud. The modest, neat houses, mostly bungalows with driveways, drifted soporifically past the window as they twisted through the suburban maze. Picturesque white signs held high on poles announced the names of the streets and eventually Mira spotted it: Belvedere Close. The car pulled in and slowed as the driver searched the numbers, stopping outside a small, square, brown brick bungalow.

"This is it," said Mira, as they stood on the pavement, the car drawing away behind them.

"Does anyone live here now?"

"I don't think so."

The curtains were closed, but other than that the house didn't stand out among the others in the street. A small driveway, a patch of grass, a low wall interrupted by a gate which opened onto a gently curving path to the brown front door.

Mira looked around but there was no one else about. Despite having the keys she felt herself a trespasser, although she was trying her best to appear at ease in front of Tom.

"Come on," she said, starting along the path towards the door.

In contrast to the brightness of the day, it was unusually dark inside. Tom closed the door behind him and the two of them stood side by side, their shoulders just touching in the narrow hallway. She felt like a little child. They both were children, their innocent touch like brother and sister. Hansel and Gretel. It was clear at once that this was no normal house, although the lack of light prevented them from seeing anything in particular to suggest it at first. There was a certain smell, not altogether unpleasant but far from domestic. Ancient and cold, like a cave. Mira moved forward and opened a door into a room, a sitting room. Her eyes were growing accustomed now and the sun pushing through the thick curtain fabric was enough to make visible the room's contents: a sofa, an armchair, a low table, a standing lamp, a small rug on the patterned carpet. Everything drab and old-fashioned but clean and somehow deliberately placed, like a museum display of how people used to live. She noticed now the walls, which had some kind of covering over them. She reached out her hand and touched it, a white plastic sheet, skin-thin, beneath which her fingers could feel the lumpen surface of the wall. A gentle tug revealed it was fixed, with pins maybe, along the top and sides of the wall, and it didn't take much more force to bring it down altogether, the whole sheet billowing jellyfish-like to the floor.

"One day he just started painting. He painted and painted and painted until all the walls were covered." She reached out her hand again and touched the surface, which gleamed like the estuarine mud. "They must have varnished it or something. It's not paint. He used food, earth, blood, anything he could lay his hands on."

Tom walked over to the other side of the room and tugged at the covering on the wall opposite, then between them they unmasked the two remaining walls, watching as the sheeting came to rest and lay like crumpled husks upon the furniture and floor. The unveiling did something to the air. It thickened. Mira felt her throat constrict and tears begin to surface, as Tom's hands reached slowly around her waist. She leaned back, letting herself soften into the circle of his embrace.

Fourteen

Jennifer didn't return to London until after Vito was gone. Their marriage continued until then as they had vowed it would. Nothing was said about that night she slipped out without a word into the cool evening air. She made something up about where she'd been. And it wasn't at all plausible of course, because who just walks out of the door one evening without saying where they're going? And she felt the knowledge that she was odd, secretive, always accompanying her whenever she was with any of the Italians who had filled her home that evening.

She kept the business going for a few more years then let it go to look after La Mamma, who could no longer be left alone. Vito carried on at his shop long after it was necessary. They had a cat and watched it grow from skittish youth to sullen old age. They religiously repainted one room of the house each year. They never went to Positano. The longer they were married the less they knew each other, what there was to be known becoming buried deeper with each passing year. They spoke of little beyond practical matters. They touched infrequently and never with intimacy. But as a partnership engaged in the unremarkable tasks of keeping a house from decay and getting an old woman from one end of the day to the other they, managed fine, excelled even, for they held no animosity towards one another. Anyone looking on would have called them happy and judged them to have attained all that a marriage could aspire to, noting perhaps the intuitive way in which they cared for each other, the small and selfless ways in which they attended to each other's comfort.

Despite their efforts to keep her at home, La Mamma was eventually admitted to the Ashton House residential care home. Her crucifix, the faded black and white photos of her parents and siblings, and her many blankets, shawls, and cloths went with her. Seeing her lying amongst them in the tiny room it was as if she inhabited her own memorial shrine. She had plenty of visitors but gave them little regard. Jennifer and Vito came most days and insisted on continuing the regular ablutions they had begun at home. With a bowl of warm water and a bar of expensive sandalwood soap between them they edged towards each other from opposite ends, Vito drawing the cloth between each misshapen toe, Jennifer stroking hers over the eyes, behind the ears, down the back of the neck, the two of them silent in respect of the quiet into which La Mamma uncharacteristically slipped during the ritual.

Together they awaited her death but it was Vito who went first. He gave her no warning. One day she walked into the sitting room with his tea and there he was slumped in his armchair, his eyes wide and vacant, a line of dribble descending from the corner of his open mouth. The television was too loud, as it always was, something about lions. She turned it off and put down the hot tea before she went to him. It was strange how calm she was, how slow and deliberate her actions. She lowered his eyelids, closed his mouth, wiped his face with a warm flannel, and gently combed his hair. Then she sat with him and held his hand, letting herself cry a little before reluctantly calling an ambulance.

He shocked everyone by choosing cremation over burial. Jennifer didn't see what all the fuss was about. They had talked about it together and she'd always thought it the best way: cleaner, neater, more final. The wood-panelled room at the crematorium was bare apart from the flowers she'd chosen, which had been brought in and placed on a table at the front. It was just herself, Paolo and Giulietta and their children, and La Mamma, who was wheeled in by a carer from Ashton House. Jennifer hadn't had any strong thoughts on music. They could barely hear it anyway above La Mamma, who wailed and crossed herself continuously. The celebrant ploughed bravely on, talking them through the events and achievements of Vito's life and likening him to a leaf, one of millions, which appears one season to flourish and then die, taking sustenance from the tree itself, which grows and endures. It was only at the end that Jennifer looked at the coffin which rested, closed, on a platform at the back of the room. Vito was inside. And then it all happened far too quickly: a curtain closed in front of it and she couldn't help it, she imagined it descending into the flames and she wanted to jump up and save him, draw him out. He wasn't a leaf. He was a man.

When presented with the ashes in the little urn she felt nothing but shame and regret, for she knew that she had failed him.

Naturally La Mamma died soon after, avoiding the indignity of a ninetieth birthday party at Ashton House. She was buried in the Catholic graveyard, lowered into the hard earth by straining coffin bearers on a cold, bleak February morning.

Giulietta, who had always had a rebellious streak, surprised them all by declaring that she preferred Vito's way. Maybe she would choose cremation herself. Paolo said it would be over his dead body and she laughed, saying it probably would. She became quite taken with the idea of where to scatter the ashes and Jennifer let her take charge, after she'd secretly taken a careful spoonful of the grey powder and placed it in the bottom of Vito's little Italian coffee pot to keep for herself.

There was talk of a trip back to Stilo and a walk up to the Basilica to let him float down gently over the village in which he was born but… no, it was far better he stay here in Southend with them. But significant locations were thin on the ground. The trouble was that Vito had never really been a fan of the outdoors. There were the cliff steps, which he and Jennifer had walked up and down most Wednesday mornings as a gesture towards keeping fit, but the routine had been far from a pleasure for him. There were his shops, the six Mr. Cobbles, and she and Giulietta agreed he would not have been displeased for a little part of him to lie down on the pavement outside each one. But with so many people traipsing past, and the road sweeper with his brush, who knew where he might end up?

Jennifer was reluctant to mention the pier, the scene of their first kiss, but they were running out of options.

"Why didn't you suggest it in the first place? It's *perfetto*!"

So they kept their eye on tide times and at around half past three one Thursday afternoon, when it was sufficiently high, they took Vito for a walk to the end of the pier, the urn wrapped in a long woollen scarf and lodged at the bottom of a green canvas shopping bag. Giulietta shrouded her head with the length of black lace she always wore for funerals, and Jennifer too wore a scarf to keep off the wind. They hadn't counted on the fishermen who colonised the end of the pier like nesting birds, forcing them to retreat to the sides for their bit of business.

They stood side by side against the rail for a moment just watching the water, and then Giulietta turned to Jennifer, the wind whipping strands of hair out from under her scarf and across her face. "Are you ready?"

"I suppose so," said Jennifer, who had been thinking how much Vito hated the wind, and the water too for that matter. She'd never once seen him swim and it was just occurring to her now that he probably couldn't. He'll drown! she thought, as Giulietta unwound the scarf from around the urn and held it carefully on top of the railings. She lifted the lid a little and a few flakes of ash rose in the wind.

"Oh!" said Jennifer, her voice emerging small and light, carried quickly away.

Giulietta quickly covered the opening with her palm. "Sorry Jenny, would you like to say a few words?"

"No," said Jennifer quickly. She wanted it over with now.

Giulietta lifted the lid once more and Jennifer reached her hand into the soft grey powder. So dry. So utterly lifeless. Yet as soon as she raised her fist above the lip of the urn it spun from her fingers as though eager to be free.

"There he goes," said Giulietta as the ashes dispersed over the muddy, churning waters.

Jennifer sold the house and moved to a one-bedroom place that was not much bigger than the bedsit she'd started off in. Not so far from it, either. It was in one of those new blocks that were going up all over the place now, built more for the young folk who caught the train to London every day than for old ladies like her, but it suited her well enough. It was new and clean, with a smooth ceramic hob and a toilet with two buttons for the flush. It had beige carpet and cream walls and bright white skirting boards and very little else. She'd carefully labelled all her furniture, wrapped and packed all her possessions, every last eggcup. But her treasures dulled in the move. Taking them out was like going through her belongings after her own death, finally seeing them for what they really were: sad, pointless, useless objects, everything either chipped or cracked or old or just plain ugly. Even the picture of Positano, which had been donated her way when Paolo sold the restaurant to a Chinese family, seemed gaudy and cheap. And her furniture, which sat around the room like misplaced boulders, seemed to sully the newness of the place. She'd persuaded a second-hand shop to come and take it all away and had bought herself a new single bed and a small sofa.

It was a nice flat, but that didn't stop her always trying to think up ways to get out of it. She still liked to walk along the seafront, and on a sunny day she took her knitting up by the bandstand. She often met Giulietta in town for a cup of tea or an ice cream, and twice a week she went to her sister-in-law's for lunch. She was really Jennifer's only friend, although anyone seeing them together could tell they were a mismatched pair: Jennifer tall and broad, Giulietta sharp and quick, taking two steps for every one of Jennifer's. That their lives had run alongside each other for so long did nothing to dispel the gulf that background, culture, and circumstance put between them. Complaining constantly about the demands her huge family made of her, Giulietta knew nothing of loneliness. And yet the two of them had found a way of being together that took no account of these things. Giulietta was there, and that was enough.

They had been on their way to East Beach to watch the controlled detonation of a World War II bomb when they came across the house. The trip was Giulietta's idea, of course, and if it hadn't been for her, Jennifer would never have entered Belvedere Close. For although East Beach remained a favourite spot of hers and she often passed by the end of that road, the sight and sound of heavy-duty machinery wouldn't have been enough to draw her off course. But Giulietta didn't even look for Jennifer's acquiescence before scurrying into the Close, so natural was her assumption that anything out of the ordinary should be properly investigated.

Orange plastic barriers had gone up around one of the properties, behind which a small crowd of onlookers was gathered. Inside the cordon a large excavator was at work, noisily digging a trench around the house, which was just a modest bungalow and looked rather lost in the middle of the moat being dug around it. There was a truck parked in the road and other workmen were involved in unloading long wooden posts from the back of it and carrying them into the property across a wobbly wooden board which bridged the trench.

"You mean you can just pick up a house and move it?"

Giulietta was already quizzing one of the bystanders, an oldish man who stood resting his arm upon the barrier as if for support.

"I don't know what they're up to. Crazy scheme. It's going to London or something," he said. And now he looked at Jennifer, for she had drawn a little closer to be included in the discussion. "It was in the paper the other day, wasn't it? Someone decided it should go into a gallery. Ha! Gonna have to be a big one! Owned by an artist it was, years ago. Been empty for years. Couple over the way used to look after the place, kept the grass mown and the house clean for the people in London what owned it."

"The Zoobs," said Jennifer.

"I don't know. Americans weren't they, more money than sense."

"Did you see it in the paper, Jenny?" asked Giulietta, craning as if to try and see in through the front door.

Jennifer had stopped taking the *Echo*. She was thinking of that woman, Grace Zoob, who had so terrified her. Her home had terrified her too, the walls crammed with all those ugly pictures. And Grace herself like an alien, with her cropped silver hair and angular features and sharp words. *I beat the shit out of him.* Those words always reared up in her mind when she thought back on that awful evening. And always when they did, the horror they aroused was always mingled with an awareness that her own flesh felt only the absence of touch. She felt it again, now. No one had touched her in such a long, long time. Even that evening, which was long before Vito died, it had been too late. Their marriage had already silently accommodated the fact that their bodies would never come together again.

"You can't just pick up a house and move it! How are they ever going to get that all the way to London?" said Giulietta, clearly thrilled by the thought.

"Beats me, but they're doing it, aren't they?" said the man. "Going by boat, apparently. They just have to get it down to the beach, then, whoosh, off it goes." He straightened up, sliding his hand out in front of him like a boat launching from the shore.

Jennifer quietly loosed herself from the conversation and began making her way around the outside of the barriers. They skirted all the way round the property which, although small, stood some distance from its neighbours, allowing this excavation to take place without much disruption to the other houses. The onlookers were not just confined to the roadside but were spread out sparsely all the way round, entering areas that would normally be deemed private property, such as the back garden. Jennifer found a gap at the rear of the bungalow and stood looking at it, although there was not much to be seen from back here, the curtains being closed as they were elsewhere and the back door firmly shut.

So this was it. She'd often wondered when out walking this way which it was, for she'd known for years that there was one around here that held her prisoner. Would she, had she come up this road, have noticed the closed curtains and suspected it? Maybe. And what would she have done then, other than to stand outside as she was now? Funnily enough, she found herself thinking of Ruth Smithson. There'd been so many girls over the years, at Keddies and then at Enid Scott's. They'd work for a year or two and then move on, and Jennifer would never hear from them again. Occasionally she'd see one in the town and it always surprised her that they'd grown old, that they weren't girls any longer. Strange how it happened. Life really was going to end, and she would probably never see inside this house. And she would probably never lose this feeling, one that she believed she'd always carried with her but which had never been stronger than it was now: that she was alone.

She struggled to retreat in her mind to a person or place with whom or where she might be comfortable. Certainly not Giulietta. Not Vito either. Not even her childhood or her parents. And she realized that she had no true friends in the world and that there was no one at all who understood anything about who she was. And it wasn't even surprising. It had always been that way. And once again the words of Grace Zoob sounded in her head: *It's not you in those paintings. This goes way beyond you. You don't matter at all.*

"Hey, Jenny, there you are!" Giulietta came hurriedly towards her. "Come on, we're going to miss the blast."

If Jennifer had told her sister-in-law what lay inside, would it have delayed her?

"It's okay, we still have fifteen minutes," she said, looking at her watch.

But by the time they made it down to the beach there were only a few minutes remaining and, there being quite a crowd, they couldn't see anything of what was going on. Jennifer was expecting some kind of warning, a countdown maybe, but they hardly had time to catch their breath before the blast, which came like a sudden attack, hitting her deep in her chest as if her heart was exploding.

Fifteen

There was a particular place, accessed down a small dark passage between two tall buildings on the north bank of the river Thames, where Ray and Pigeon could sit unseen on a kind of small stone platform, a jetty almost, close to the water that lapped at the steps below. They spent much of their time by the river. It provided a natural focus to an otherwise aimless existence, and the choice of bridges was good for nesting down at night. But, even so, Pigeon had always been wary of the water and on the occasions when they came here to this old, hidden-away jetty, she wouldn't get too close, settling down a cautious distance from the edge. Ray, on the other hand, liked being near the river and would sit as he was now with his legs dangling over the side of the wall, his heels kicking gently against the algae-covered stones, his gaze lowered to the brown river, caught up in the patterns it made as it flowed past, the small splashes as it slapped against the wall.

Maybe it was this distance between them which always fostered in Ray an unusual level of introspection at the times he came to this spot. Life on the streets had done much to shut down those parts of his brain not concerned with basic survival, concerns he found increasingly wearying, as if his stomach should by now have learned to do without food entirely rather than be constantly gnawing away at him, never satisfied by what he managed to throw at it. And there was Pigeon to worry about too, who looked to him as provider and whose dependency Ray felt keenly. Despite the bird being an adept scavenger, Ray knew that, one-eyed and unable to fly, she would never have survived this long alone.

But sitting here in this dank, solitary spot with Pigeon squatting quietly behind him released him for a time from the pressures of his existence. Sometimes he could sit for a long while without awareness of anything passing through his mind at all. But often he fell to thinking a little of his past. Of his years in Southend perhaps. A few memories of that earlier life had been given back to him. Enough for him to realize that it was not worth trying to resume it. He remembered less from those interim years with the Zoobs, which were shrouded by an almost impenetrable fog. Were it not for this "almost," these thoughtful times by the river might have been limited to recollections of those occasions when, as a boy, he'd found some moment of companionship with, say, a trail of ants marching towards his own kindly placed segment of orange, or a snail making its slow course towards a lettuce leaf offering. But there were chinks in the veil of forgetfulness and some of what was intimated through it troubled him a great deal.

One of the things that had continued to worry him over the years was the vague but niggling awareness that there had been someone important who was now lost to him. And now, as he had on many previous occasions, he tried to search his mind for some further clue as to who she might be. He knew her to be a woman, although this in itself was strange to him as he also knew himself to be someone who didn't have relationships with women. There had been the early infatuation with Louise, and he had had the occasional friendship over the years which, for a brief time, had developed the potential to become something more. He remembered one girl in particular, a girl who worked in the canteen at the Civic Centre, who had surprised him by asking him to go rowing on the boating lake one weekend. But their acquaintance hadn't gone beyond a couple of outings and the most reticent of kisses, and he knew it couldn't be she who was troubling him now. No, this woman had been someone deeply important to him. He hardly dared to think it, and yet he felt it must be true: she was someone with whom he had been very much in love. Indeed, he felt he must be still, for his heart ached just to ponder the possibility. And yet how could he be in love with someone whose name he couldn't even remember? He really couldn't recall a single thing about her, hardly even her face, beyond the conviction that she did *have* a face and was not merely a figment of his imagination.

The more often he thought on it the more certain he became that he had known love and had lost it. How it had come upon him or who had been the focus of it remained a mystery, but today something new occurred to him: that there might be a connection between this person and something else he could never quite get to the bottom of. For a while now he'd had the feeling that during those now-misty years with the Zoobs he'd been engaged in some very important task. Something which he had either chosen or been forced to abandon. There was something that he had been trying to achieve and yet, when he tried to think back as to what it might have been, all he could remember doing was painting pictures. Why on earth had he been painting pictures when there was clearly something pressing and far more important he needed to do? It was a task, he felt certain, that someone had entrusted to him and it occurred to him now that maybe it was something he'd been doing for her. Or, if not, that it was at least connected to her in some way. Had he, perhaps, been trying to find her? If he could just remember what the task was he might even now be able to fulfil it.

As he sat there looking into the river it seemed to him as if he might be making a little progress, as if his mind, like the muddy brown water below, might suddenly clear and everything would make sense.

Maybe it was these thoughts, coupled with the dreamy state he was in, which accounted for his lack of surprise at what he saw when he glanced up from his reverie: it was his old house, the bungalow in Shoeburyness. Just floating past down the river. Despite his many years away from it and the vagaries of his memory, he recognised it at once, as clearly as if he had been walking into Belvedere Close in search of it. And not only was it not surprising to him to see it here upon the Thames, but, appearing now amid these thoughts, it seemed to him as if it might actually be coming to meet him, providing the clarity which he'd felt just a moment before to be almost within his grasp.

For the first time in many years he felt a quickening within. He was buoyant, elated almost, and instinctively looked behind him for his companion. Scooping Pigeon up, he carried her onto his lap. The bird's little heart raced to be brought so close to the water but Ray held her firm, with both hands cupping her breast until slowly the beat settled to its usual fast but steady pace. *Do you see that, Pidge? That's my house. Right there. If we can just get across to it I'll show it to you. If only we could fly. If we could fly, Pidge, I'd take you there right now.*

Sixteen

Jennifer watched the list of stations scroll along the board on the station platform, the places she'd known her whole life—Chalkwell, Leigh-on-Sea, Benfleet—linked by casual little commas to foreign, far off destinations—Limehouse, London Fenchurch Street—as if they were all just stitches on the same row of knitting and going from one to the other was perfectly simple and natural. Plenty of people did this journey every day and Jennifer was not such a stranger to it as she might have been, as she'd taken the same trip with Giulietta just six months before, when Paola had taken them to see *Les Miserables* for Jennifer's seventieth birthday. And there was that other occasion of course, a long time ago now, when she had sat nervously next to that young journalist. But she was trying not to think about that.

As she stood waiting she reached inside her bag and felt for the little silver coffee pot she'd brought with her. It was the pot, rather than its contents, which had come to stand in for her husband in her mind. It had even started to look a little like him: the steel was marked here and there by darkened blotches like the liver spots on his hands and forehead, and the spout's lower lip, protruding in a sweet and vulnerable sort of a way, was reminiscent of an expression that he would wear when trying to solicit a kiss.

Slowly and unapologetically the train pulled in, eleven minutes late. There were plenty of seats: in fact, the carriage was practically empty. She chose one of a pair facing forward and put her handbag, with Vito in it, carefully down on the seat beside her. She occupied herself with the view from the window as they crossed the railway bridge over the High Street, full already with shoppers, and on past Old Leigh where dinghies were marooned in the glistening mud of the estuary. Soon they were racing through the flat, sparsely industrialized Essex landscape which spun past her, hardly registering on the senses at all, putting her into a kind of trance.

Recovering herself as they drew closer towards the city she turned away from the window and reached across to her handbag, pulling out the newspaper cutting she'd carefully folded and tucked into the inner pocket. After that day when she and Giulietta had been to watch the bomb explode she'd begun buying a national newspaper daily, trawling the Arts and Culture section in the hope of spotting something. And one day, there it was: *8 Belvedere Close, Turbine Hall, Tate Modern, London.*

The first major work by Outsider Artist Ray Eccles—his own 1970s bungalow—is here resurrected and exhibited for the first time, having been removed and transported from its plot in Belvedere Close, Southend-on-Sea, by Mira Zoob, daughter of the late Outsider Art collectors, George and Grace Zoob. This was the birthplace of Eccles' famous She series, an image of a woman standing on a beach, which he began to paint obsessively on the walls of his house in materials ranging from soup to his own bodily fluids, many of which have sadly not withstood the test of time or transportation. The woman's face, with its enigmatic stare, has become one of the iconic images of 20th century art, although viewers will be taken aback by the power and immediacy of these first crazed depictions. Inside the vast industrial space of the Turbine Hall, 8 Belvedere Close takes on the feel of a simulacrum and the setting offers some interesting juxtapositions: the unchecked artistic imagination inside the shell of identikit 70s suburban architecture, inside the shell of the cathedral to modern art. The lighting, designed to mimic daylight, and a background soundtrack of squawking seagulls are meant to enhance the experience but are an unnecessary gimmick. Still, not to be missed.

When the train pulled into Fenchurch Street station Jennifer had half a mind to stay on it and be taken straight back to Westcliff. The platform was dark and gloomy, full of menace and noise: engines, whistles, hurried footsteps, and announcements following relentlessly one after another. But she wouldn't have gotten this far if she hadn't gotten used to bullying herself out of these little inertias.

"Last stop, lady," said a litter-picker gruffly as he passed by her seat, and she quickly collected her belongings and exited the train onto the platform.

She looked around for an escape route and joined the flow of people disappearing down a flight of steps. They led down into a ticket hall and a row of barriers, on the other side of which she found a map showing directions to the underground station at Tower Hill.

She resurfaced from the Tube at Blackfriars, having decided beforehand against changing lines, and asked directions of a tall young man casually leaning against the wall at the station entrance. He straightened up, crossed his arms and looked into the distance with a frown.

"Oh dear, is it very far?" said Jennifer.

"No, not really," he said with an amused smile. "Ten minutes? But it's a lovely walk… across the river." He pointed up the street to their right, at the top of which could be made out the edge of St. Paul's Cathedral. Once she got there, he told her, it was quite simple, she just needed to head directly south across the river over the footbridge.

"Good luck!" he called after her, and when she glanced round she saw he'd been joined by a girl, who smiled and waved as well.

The cathedral was being cleaned. The bottom part of one side was covered in scaffolding, which was itself covered with a huge piece of cloth printed with a photograph of the obscured section. Above, the already-cleaned stones were smooth and pale; beneath, the road was clogged with cars and buses churning out their muck as though in defiance of the whole operation. Jennifer stood for a moment catching her breath, craning her neck to see right to the very top where a little gilt cross shone, poking its way free into the high narrow sky above the city. Across the other side of the road she spotted the young man and his girl striding briskly together, his long arm slung loosely around her shoulder. They swung right, down a wide walkway that opened up towards the river, and she watched them for a while, their heads bobbing with conversation and kisses, before she lost them among the ripple of pedestrians making the trip south.

She crossed the road and climbed the wide, shallow steps that rose from the side of the walkway to get a better view of where she was heading. She could see the footbridge now, a slender white aisle shooting out into nothing between the brick buildings. With the cold pale sun shining thinly upon it, it seemed made of ice or densely packed snow. She watched the stream of people crowd on and disappear over the hump, so many of them, like refugees. Beyond, as if blocking their passage and their dreams, was a vast brick building, windowless and ugly like a prison. Big black letters stamped high across the top spelled out the name of the gallery: TATE MODERN COLLECTION. She glanced back at the cathedral with its high dome, smooth and secretive, and again at the gallery, unrelenting on the other side of the river. The two buildings seemed to be engaged in a staring contest.

There weren't nearly as many people on the bridge as there had seemed from farther back. And it wasn't made of ice or anything so elegant, but steel planks that clanked a little underfoot. She paused for a moment in the middle, amazed to see the whole city suddenly laid clear, the river opening up down the centre like a huge zip. The Thames was wider than she'd ever imagined, the water muddy and lively, bobbing with bits of litter which, moving with so much pace and certainty, seemed an almost decorative touch. Pleasure boats with rows of empty plastic seats on their open decks charged underneath, and further down the river she could see Tower Bridge, small and spotless like a toy model of itself.

Closer now, she could see the whole of the gallery and a number of other names stamped across the top. Her eyes went straight to the one she knew: ECCLES. How stern and accusing those letters seemed, bold and separate like a row of black crows peering down from a telegraph wire. What was she doing here? She couldn't see that any good would come from going any further. But to turn back… to stand still… sometimes you just had to put one foot in front of the other and tell yourself that you'd have a nice cup of tea when you got home.

She entered the gallery down a wide concrete slope that continued its downward progression once inside the building, the rough surface turning smooth and polished under the high roof. To her left, on a lower, warmly-illuminated level, people browsed and bought things in a bookshop, and high above her head black steel beams criss-crossed a narrow strip of dull white daylight that ran the length of the building. She paused, letting people pass by on either side of her on their way down the ramp. Their feet made soft echoes and squeaks on the polished concrete, their voices small like the chirrups of garden birds against the low background hum. Ahead, at the bottom of the slope, was a sort of bridge from which people peered lazily down as if into a meandering stream. Emerging from underneath she saw the house: number eight Belvedere Close.

Suddenly she felt very nervous, as if she were arriving to meet someone—as if he were in there, waiting—and terribly conscious of her appearance, which was presentable, of course: she'd chosen her clothes carefully for the trip, and had a pretty scarf around her neck with a pattern of doves and blossom. But there was no escaping her age: her grey hair, which needed hairspray to behave, and her strange lined skin. All those things that had crept up to obscure what was beneath, like dust on an old forgotten painting.

She clutched her handbag and pulled her coat around her, telling herself how silly she was being. No one was waiting for her. No one even knew or cared that she'd arrived. In this vast, grey space, the bungalow was like a dolls' house in an attic, the little people that had once been given life inside long since forgotten and discarded. She walked a little closer and stood behind the rope barrier that had been erected around the outside, beyond which was a low wall bordering a parched patch of grass, a pink hydrangea bush poking over the top of the bricks. Was it real? She reached out and touched a flower head. It felt dry and thin under her hand, like tissue paper, but when she plucked a petal and pressed it into her fingertip it bruised and bled the faintest trace of moisture.

The queue to get inside trailed all the way down the path and beyond the barrier. She made her way to the end. Waiting in line she heard the seagull sounds coming from high above her head, as though the birds were circling in the steel rafters. She lifted her face and it met the hot beam of a spotlight. She closed her eyes as if warming herself in the sun, until she felt a light touch on her shoulder and looked down to see a gap had opened up in the queue.

There was a strange smell inside. Peaty and sour, like wet coals. People huddled in the narrow hall which, after the huge hangar-like space of the gallery, seemed unreasonably small and dark. Other bodies brushed against her own, their whispers and shuffling feet forming a tight conspiratorial circle around her. Dizzy and confused, she pressed her way through towards an open doorway to her right and, entering the room, she found the arm of a settee upon which to rest, for she felt she might otherwise collapse.

"No sitting on the furniture, please," called a voice from the other side of the room.

She stood up again immediately, looking around for where the instruction had come from and finding a girl with her legs crossed on a low stool in the corner of the room, a pool of yellow light surrounding her from the tassel-shaded standing lamp above her head.

"I'm sorry," mouthed Jennifer, bowing her head in apology and moving towards the centre of the room.

She stood for a moment, trying to recover herself. There were about ten others in the room. They moved about the space slowly, like unhappy zoo animals, pacing the outskirts of the room and looking at the walls in a puzzled way, as if trying to find a way out. Again, Jennifer was struck by a feeling of panic, of not knowing what she was doing here, or how to behave now that she was. And she felt rather exposed, as if she must stand out in some way. What if she were recognized? Surely it was possible. Seeking a less conspicuous spot, she made her way to towards the outskirts of the room to join the flow. And then she finally let her gaze fall upon the walls.

She had expected to know herself better. She had geared up for this trip as if going to meet herself. Herself as she really was. These walls seemed at first glance to be covered in dirt, as if dredged from the bottom of a canal. They were so dark, and shiny, as if wet. But as she continued to stare at them, eyes emerged ghost-like through the mire and, as she stepped back a little way, a whole face came slowly into view. Coming to meet her, these strange, shy shadows of herself. Or rather, she was going to meet them, being lowered into their underwater world: dark, silent, and strange.

She turned in a slow circle, moving her gaze around the room, and as she did so it seemed to wrap itself around her, closer and closer until she felt herself held in its embrace. *It's not you in those paintings. You don't matter at all.* It was a lie. It was her. And she did matter. She felt her flesh caressed, waking up. It was intimate but comforting, with no edge of menace. She was not afraid. Even though her blood had never pounded with such ferocity through her body, as if it wanted to be free.

She had no awareness now of the other people in the room. It seemed to belong entirely to her.

"So sorry, I didn't mean to alarm you."

She looked up to see a large face, ruddy and bearded. A heavy hand on her shoulder. "It's just you look as enthralled as I am. It's disconcerting, don't you think, the way she looks at you? Those large, dark eyes. It's like she lived a long, long time ago. *Way* back. Like those ancient Egyptian portraits. Did you ever get the chance to see them? I forget what they're called but they were dug up from a graveyard somewhere. Painted to adorn mummies, I think, to accompany their owners to the afterlife. They're so compelling, like you're really coming face to face with someone who lived thousands of years ago. I don't know about this woman. She may still be alive. But she looks ancient to me, kind of wise and sad. Like she knows something we don't."

"I—" Jennifer started to speak although she had no words to follow it with. She felt suddenly hot and suffocated, unable to breathe. "I'm sorry, I— I really must go."

She walked fast, almost running from the room, pushing past people in the hall, looking desperately for a way out, for air. She found the back door and emerged, breathless, into the small garden, just a patch of dry grass. Beyond it the smooth floor of the gallery continued, empty, until it hit the rear wall, and she let her eyes and her mind rest there for a moment in the space and the blankness.

She couldn't possibly go back in. So she walked round to the front of the bungalow, and without looking behind her, she made her way back up the ramp, very much in need of somewhere to sit. Plenty had made do with the floor. A few even lay down, looking up at the ceiling. But as for a chair or a bench there was nothing. She carried on outside, walking around to the front of the building and across the wide forecourt. Rows of silver birch were planted close together in slim rectangular beds like miniature forests, and their leaves hissed together in the breeze. The air smelt of onions, and she saw there was a cart selling hot dogs just beyond the trees. As she approached she could hear the sizzle and saw at last her place to sit: a single wooden bench, positioned on the far side of the wide walkway that ran alongside the river, just behind the railings.

From here the bridge she'd walked over looked long and delicate, strung out across the water like a spine, and on the other side she could still see the reassuring dome of St. Paul's. Behind the long line of riverfront buildings were many tall yellow cranes, like city-dwelling giraffes chomping at the small clouds that had formed in a uniform line along the tops of the buildings. She reached into her handbag and drew out her knitting. It was the time of year when she should have been thinking about Christmas presents but instead she'd gotten started on a cardigan for Francesca's little one. She'd chosen a special yarn with a little cashmere in it, in purest white, each ball light like something that should be lifted and carried on a warm summertime breeze. She paused before drawing it out, letting her hand rest for a minute in the innocent softness. It was strange—she felt a lot like crying.

She looked ahead, through the railings at the river. The water was pale brown. It moved quickly, a slight silkiness to the waves and ripples. She stared at it for a while, at the shapes that swam and dipped and morphed across the surface. Borne upon them were remnants of the emotions stirred within her in the bungalow, the feeling that at long last she had been touched, known. And now she just felt very sad, there was no getting away from it. She was sad that Vito was dead. That their chance at being alive together was over.

But it wouldn't help anyone, letting her thoughts float around like that. She pulled out the wool and her needles from the bag. The few rows she'd completed were huddled along one of them in that pathetic way that always disheartened her at the start of a new project. She wound the yarn around her little finger, nestled each needle into the hollow behind her thumbs, and, slowly at first, began to knit. The river was just a noise now, the occasional swoosh of boats on their way past, and there were other noises behind: the clicking of heels on the walkway, the tick-ticking of bicycle wheels, all carrying on around her as she settled her mind into the slow rhythm of the stitches.

She saw, after a time, that someone had sat down next to her. It was in a glance to her right—drawing out a little more yarn from the bag—that she saw the pair of long, thin, black-stockinged legs, one crossed over the other. At their end, the toes just shy of the railings, was a pair of royal blue patent leather shoes. And next to her bag there was now a hand. It was the hand that delayed her, just for a moment, from starting her next row, for it was curiously placed: flat on the seat of the bench, the fingers spaced a little apart as if presenting itself to her view. It was a young hand, pale, long-fingered and delicate. The knuckles were pink, the skin blotched a little by the cold, the nails chewed down well below the fingertips and the skin around them dotted with tender little cuts. It seemed to quiver slightly, a frail and vulnerable thing, and as she looked at it there arose from somewhere a strange thought, not so much a thought even, but an impulse: to touch it.

She fought against it, of course she did, but something was urging her on. And she somehow knew that were she to do it, were she to lay her own hand down gently upon this other one, the world would change, just a little bit. For perhaps the first time in her life she felt it was in her power to make something happen, to change her own course of events, which had seemed, just a moment ago as she'd sat staring into the Thames, destined to carry on their strange churning way to the grave with no resolution, no sense. Here she'd sat, as compliant as water, and yet here now was a spark of rebellion, gathering in her right hand. She had only to surrender to it and…

But at that moment the hand moved. Just like that, as if it had been blown by a sudden gust of wind.

It had disappeared into the pocket of a short, black jacket to draw out a packet of cigarettes and a lighter. Mira Zoob was cold. But she didn't want to go inside, not yet anyway. She'd worked for two years to get it shown, but the little bungalow depressed her, seeing all those people crawling over it like flies. Tom was bringing his mother to see it but had rung to say they were going to be late. She lit the cigarette and drew the smoke deep inside her. She imagined, as she often did, it entering and filling the labyrinthine passages and cavities of her lungs. When she breathed it out she liked to think that it held their shape for a moment, lace-like, before dispersing in the air. The old woman beside her on the bench had stopped her knitting and was putting it away in her bag. Mira watched the mottled, reptilian hands with curiosity, regarding them as she might a creature in a zoo rather than as an image of what her own skin would one day become. They moved slowly, foraging about in the soft leather bag, then drawing something out, a dull metal object. It was a small Italian coffee pot. Mira became conscious that she was staring and looked away, drawing upon her cigarette and blowing out a thin cloud of smoke in the opposite direction. She flicked the ash upon the floor, staring down at the tiny nuggets of shattered glass that lay about the foot of the bench. And then she glanced again to her left.

The old woman was now holding the coffee pot in her lap, both hands resting upon it with a kind of pacifying tenderness, as if it was a rabbit that might bolt. Then she lifted it up and began, very slowly and carefully, to unscrew the bottom from the top. She put the top half down on the bench beside her to her left, out of Mira's sight, but drew the bottom portion close to her chest, cupping her hand over the top as if protecting it from the wind. Mira sat up a little straighter to try and see what was inside but the woman was holding it higher now, close under her chin, making it impossible to see in without overtly peering. There *was* something inside though, that much was clear, for the woman kept glancing down into it and kept her hand protectively over the opening. Then she touched the index finger of her other hand to her tongue, reached it carefully, almost trepidatiously, into the pot, and, after a moment, drew it out. Mira didn't have a chance to see what lay on her fingertip, for the woman transferred it swiftly to her mouth, keeping her finger gripped softly between her teeth as if depositing something gently and purposefully upon her tongue.

Mira got up. She felt suddenly as if she was intruding upon some terribly intimate act, some strange and private ritual. But also, for the first time in… perhaps for the first time ever, she'd felt something come alive in her mind, the start of an idea, and by leaving now, abruptly, she felt she might catch it, preserve it, before it merged and dissipated into the day. She'd wasted her time at college on sculptures involving dismembered dolls. The theme had drifted on into the start of her third year and she'd been thinking of dropping out. It was all so empty, so wildly unoriginal. But there was something about that little coffee pot, the tenderness of the hands upon it… She wouldn't think any more about it, she wouldn't force it, but put it away at the back of her mind to germinate and grow.

She walked round behind the bench and started out across the forecourt towards the entrance of the gallery. There were still twenty minutes before she was due to meet Tom and his mother at the foot of the Millennium Bridge. She entered through the automatic doors, walked past the shop and on through another set of glass doors into the gallery proper. She wandered onto the bridge that spanned the Turbine Hall and, in the centre, stopped to lean against the rail, peering down onto the roof of the bungalow. She looked one by one at the faces of those who stood in the queue to get inside. There was always the faint hope that he would be among them and she felt certain that if he was she would know him instantly, even though she remembered Ray Eccles only in the vaguest of terms, with the intangible fondness with which one might recall a childhood imaginary friend. As the run of the exhibit drew on and the likelihood of him turning up dwindled, she felt the emptiness of disappointment settling. She didn't always admit to herself that finding the man she'd become convinced was her father was what this whole project had been about. But even in interviews with the press she'd acknowledged that the thought had crossed her mind: that he might show up to see the bungalow, that he might make himself known to her, if only out of curiosity. There'd been plenty of publicity. If he was alive he would have heard about it. If he'd wanted to find her he would have done so by now.

She wished she could remember more about her childhood. She wished she knew more about where she came from. There was no one left now to fill in the gaps. There was so much that she didn't know and would never know. She was always telling Tom to talk to his parents about the past while he still had the chance. Had they been happy? Had they truly loved each other? Did they have regrets? He just laughed at her, telling her he didn't need to know all that. But he had no idea how it felt to be all alone like her, set adrift like a little boat upon the deep dark sea.

She looked at her watch: there was still time. She would go and see a painting that she hadn't seen for years. It was on the third floor. She took the escalator. Away from the shop and the Turbine Hall, the gallery was much quieter. She walked slowly through the rooms until she came to the du Feu. *Group, sitting* had a whole wall to itself and she stood herself squarely in front of it. Two women had followed her in and she listened to their one-word judgements as they circled the room. "Creepy," said one when they arrived next to Mira, and then they moved on.

Mira looked for a long time at the little girl lying on the floor in her tutu and her red wellies. Trying to figure her out. Trying, somehow, to get her attention. But it was no good. The look in her eyes was too sad and too distant.

As if she knew what was coming and had decided to give up there and then, just lie down on the floor and wait for it all to be over.

Outside, the air was alive with birdsong: Korean men were playing little wooden whistles by the foot of the bridge. Mira paced directionless around the forecourt, glancing now and then at the faces of the people coming over the bridge, searching for Tom. She was looking forward to seeing him, to kissing his lips, always so plump and smooth. She wished he was coming alone, without his mother. She wanted to talk to him. Their time together so far had been dominated by the planning of this exhibition and he'd been much involved, especially with the logistics of getting it here. The whole thing had cost a fortune, but she didn't care about that. They'd stood together on the banks of the Thames watching it sail through an open Tower Bridge, the traffic stopped for the bungalow tied to its floating platform. And then they'd followed it hand in hand, half running, excited as a couple of children as it made its way upriver towards the gallery. She'd felt the pride and elation passing between them, uniting them, for only they knew of all the obstacles that had been overcome to make this moment possible. But now she was ready for more. She wanted really to know him, and to be known. How could she tell him that? She would try.

Her attention was caught by a homeless man standing beneath one of the posters for 8 Belvedere Close displayed in a large lollipop-like structure planted in the concrete outside the gallery. She always noticed such people. She felt an affinity with tramps and beggars, people without a place in the world, and always stopped to give them money. Although money was so inadequate as a gift. She gave it and she smiled but it failed to communicate any of the companionship she felt. This man wasn't asking for money though. He seemed to be genuinely interested in the poster. She ambled closer, wondering what it was about him exactly that made her immediately assume he was homeless. For if you examined his clothing it was actually kind of smart, or at least had been once. He wore a dark suit jacket, a little too big but not ill fitting, though admittedly it was dusty and shabby and had holes in the elbows. The trousers appeared to match and as she moved round the other side of the structure she could see he was even wearing a dishevelled tie, the silvery threads frayed and fluttering free. He was tall and thin; there was something almost elegant about him. Even his grey hair, hanging long, sparse and straggly on either side of his bald head, lent him a kind of weary dignity, as did his unkempt beard which blew softly in the wind like sheep's wool caught on barbed wire. He was bobbing his head in a strange rhythmical fashion, some kind of nervous tic, she assumed, and had one hand in his pocket, the arm bent and slightly tensed as if he were gripping something in there.

"You should go in and take a look," she said, moving round to his side of the display board, looking up at it with him. "It's free."

He looked at her but said nothing, and after a few further moments of silence she assumed that he hadn't understood her. She was about to try again when she felt a hand on her shoulder and turned round to see Tom. He kissed her quickly.

"Sorry we're late."

"My fault," said his mother, "there was some problem with the trains."

She also gave Mira a kiss on the cheek, keeping a hand resting on her shoulder for a moment after it was given.

"How *are* you?" The sun was in her eyes, causing her to squint a little, an expression that emphasized the scrutiny Mira always felt under in her company. Concern for her son, that he should be caught up with someone carrying so much pain.

"I'm good," said Mira lightly. "I'm afraid there isn't much time now though, the gallery closes at six."

"Let's get going then," said Tom's mother, turning and setting off briskly towards the entrance.

Mira and Tom followed and, to her surprise, the homeless man turned too, following just a couple of steps behind. Mira turned to him. "Yes," she said, smiling at him and gesturing towards the gallery. "Come."

Tom took her hand and pulled her close. "Where did you find *him*?" he whispered into her ear.

Mira put a finger to her lips. "Don't worry," she whispered, "he's harmless."

"But who is he? What's he doing with us?" he persisted, and Mira let go of his hand, feeling his questions opening up a distance between them.

"Shhh," she said, turning to check that the man was still following them.

"We've got Mum here, remember," said Tom, walking a little ahead to catch up with her.

The four of them stood on the bridge looking down at the bungalow: Tom's mother was between him and Mira, the homeless man next to Mira on the other side, a little removed from the three of them but clearly waiting with them. He still hadn't said a word, but as they stood there Mira could hear he was making a soft sound, a kind of humming. She glanced sideways at him, free to examine his face as he stared, seemingly absorbed, at the bungalow. The lights from the rafters caught his eyes, lost almost entirely in the folds of his skin so that they were simply little specks of reflected light, so sharp and bright that there could only be tears within.

"It looks so small," said Tom's mother.

"Yes," said Mira, turning her attention to the bungalow. Looking at it now it did, strangely, appear different, smaller in some way. She found herself recalling her mother, her body lying flat and demure on its back in the undertaker's chapel. The ravaged look that cancer had given her was gone completely. She was small and serene, like a little doll. Pretty, almost. So much more delicate and vulnerable than Mira had ever known her to be. The little house below appeared somehow similar, lying on the smooth concrete floor as if on a slab at the morgue, people poring over it as if all boundaries of personal space had collapsed. But how fragile, how sweet it looked. All those little tiles on the roof, and the little brown bricks too. The front door, the windows, the guttering running all the way round. It was so perfect, and yet too late somehow for its perfection to be of any use.

She could hear Tom talking to his mother about it and felt relieved that she wasn't having to do so herself. She was so tired of talking to people about it.

"Yep, just a normal guy, and then one day he just starts painting."

"I wonder why."

"We don't know. But these are the very first paintings he did of the woman on the beach. He used anything he had in the house back then. Food, all sorts."

"Shall we go down?" said Mira.

She held back, letting Tom and his mum take the lead down the steps, then touched the old man lightly on his arm, gesturing for him to follow her.

"We're closing in ten minutes," the steward sitting at the front door told them as they approached.

"It's okay, we won't be long," said Mira. Taking Tom's hand, she stepped over the threshold, turning to check that the old man was still behind them. She stepped forward, giving him room to enter, and watched him wipe his feet purposefully back and forth on the mat, then step slowly and carefully into the hallway. He closed his eyes and appeared to be smelling the air, making her aware of it too, the lingering traces of unknown bodies. She let Tom's hand drop and he walked off into the sitting room. She knew he was cross and confused that her attention was so absorbed by this stranger, that she wasn't being the guide to his mother that he wanted her to be. But she didn't care. He could talk to his mother, answer all her silly questions. He liked talking about it. He talked about it as if it was his own. But it didn't belong to him. It was hers. And she wanted to offer it as a gift to this poor old man.

He too walked past her and through into the sitting room, and she followed, watching for his reaction. But he seemed more interested in the furniture than what was on the walls. His hand brushed lightly over the arm of the sofa, he looked down at the floor, his foot slowly and carefully following the swirl of the pattern in the carpet. Then he walked over to the window and stood looking out, as if upon a wide vista rather than just the interior of the gallery. She stood quite close to him but he didn't seem aware of her presence at all. After a time he looked away from the window and down at his hand. He held it out, palm upwards, and appeared to be studying it, a puzzled, melancholy expression on his face. The other hand remained in his pocket, and his head still bobbed backwards and forwards in that curious manner. Then suddenly his hand fell to his side and he turned and walked out of the room. She thought he must be leaving and felt a terrible disappointment that what he'd seen had failed to touch him in any way. And yet when she followed she saw that he went not towards the back door but into the small bedroom on the opposite side of the hallway.

The narrow single bed was positioned along the wall beneath the window on the far side of the room and he walked directly to it, standing over it for a short while before lowering himself down to sit on the edge.

The steward who was seated just inside the door rose immediately from her stool.

"No sitting on—"

"Let him," interrupted Mira. "It's okay."

She stood at the doorway and watched as the thin, stiff body eased itself back onto the bed, the legs swinging up with a slow mechanical grace, the head lowering down towards the pillow. His movements were restricted somewhat by only having the aid of one hand, the other remaining at all times in his pocket in a way that made her wonder if he might be missing the other and concealing a stump. With his able hand he drew the meagre covers out from where they were tucked under the mattress and manoeuvred himself beneath them, turning his back to her as he tucked his knees up to his chest in a fetal curl.

The steward looked again at Mira, concerned.

"Honestly, it's fine," she said, walking over towards the bed. He had his eyes closed and she lowered her hand, thinking now she might touch him, stroke the frail strands of grey hair that fell over his forehead. He was like a child lying there, a strange old child. She felt, looking down at him, that her gift had been received.

"It's just that we're about to close up," said the steward, getting up from her stool.

"I know," said Mira, turning. "But don't wake him. Don't wake him just yet."

*

He'd seen his house floating down the river and had followed it here. He had watched it lifted high in the air, swaying this way and that before coming slowly to rest on the back of a flatbed truck, a huge platform on wheels. He'd watched it disappear inside the vast brick building and had not followed it any further, for although he saw people freely coming and going, pouring in and out of the wide glass doors, he'd spent too long outside the company of others to feel any right to be among them. So he'd stayed outside with the birds, scavenging the remains of half-eaten hot dogs once the crowds had cleared and using their polystyrene containers to piece together a makeshift mattress beneath the footbridge.

But then one day a girl had spoken to him. She had invited him in. Maybe her face stirred a memory within him of a child with dark curls, milk-white skin, and raspberry lips. Maybe it was this that persuaded him to accept the invitation, to follow her through the doors that parted smoothly to let her enter. He stood beside her, not too close, for his skin bristled to be near a creature so smooth and youthful. There below them was his home. No ropes or wheels or platforms now. Just sitting there in the middle of a huge grey space. And his bones ached with longing to be inside, to rest.

And yet when he'd entered the bungalow he'd discovered such a mess. Such filth. Upon the walls, everywhere. Worse than the pigeon excrement he'd become accustomed to sleeping on, to having on his own person. Far worse, because this was all his own doing. It was true: he had been painting and he realized with shame that this was the result. But standing here, too humiliated to take Pigeon out of his pocket to see the house in which he'd once lived, he found himself recalling what it was he'd really been trying to do. He'd been trying to fly. And somehow he had been persuaded of the lunatic belief that he could do it.

If that sounds crazy, then I suspect you have not seen the paintings themselves. For anyone who has, and has been touched by their beauty, will surely recognize the truth of it: that what you are seeing is not just a woman standing on a beach, but a spirit soaring, a man attempting to fly. He took up a paintbrush and tried to find wings. For it was never just a painting to him. It was a hope. A hope that swelled then died with the final brushstroke.

Exactly what occurred that day on East Beach remains a mystery even to him. Struck by a dying bird; his eye momentarily made use of. He saw something and had no choice but to respond. In love, yes. In love like a fish is in water. So that now, lifted out of it, he has no real memory of what it was like to live and breathe in that medium, but is left only with a sense of lacking, a sad shrinking kind of feeling he doesn't fully recognize as regret. But the little bed in the corner of the room offers him the rest he craves. Not just rest, but forgiveness. For all his audacity and his failure he is forgiven. Vindicated even, for as he pulls the blanket up under his chin he can feel his arm twitching, in readiness for flight. And he can sense a face coming out of the shadows to meet him. Maybe he will really do it this time. And maybe when he does he will see her again. He closes his eyes and feels the bungalow slip its moorings. Set adrift. Floating back down the wide brown river, all the way home.

Reading guide

1. Ray is a cryptic character, especially for a protagonist. As readers, do we ever truly know him?

2. Early in the book, Ray is described as being "past the age when anything interesting was likely to happen to him." The same might be said of Jennifer when we rejoin her in Chapter 6—the moment when something extremely interesting happens to her. What do you think the author is trying to tell us via the similarities of these characters, and what else do they have in common?

3. Ray has, to say the least, an unorthodox relationship with George and Grace. But right up until Grace turns violent, it never seems to affect Ray's art. What do you think this says about the couple's interest in him—or about the art itself?

4. The main characters have very little interaction. This is particularly drawn into focus at the end, where Ray and Jennifer very nearly meet and interact, but then miss each other. Why do you think the author ends the book with this missed connection?

5. At the end of the novel, the narrator addresses the reader, writing of Ray's aspirations, "If that sounds crazy to you,

then I suspect you have not seen the paintings themselves. For anyone who has, and has been touched by their beauty, will surely recognise the truth of it: that what you are seeing is not just a woman standing on a beach, but a spirit soaring, a man attempting to fly." Having not seen the fictive paintings, does it sound "crazy" to you? Do you think Ray achieves flight—and, if so, what kind?

6. If you could ask the author one question, what would it be?

About the Book:
An Interview with Harriet Paige

Why, of all possible birds, a seagull?

A gull is a very common bird, but also possesses great beauty. When I see them up close, their beauty always surprises me; the white of the feathers that run over the head and breast is so pure it possesses a kind of lustre and richness. That suited the theme of transcendence within the everyday. Seagulls also have a very piercing gaze, a kind of knowing look, which suited me too. I wanted the accident on the beach to have a fatalistic aspect, as if Ray was being chosen, honed in on.

This is an unusual book, by turns absurdist and deeply felt. Could you talk a bit about its origins?

In my recollection the seed for the idea was planted when I heard someone talking on the radio about the importance of forgetting. That if we were to retain everything that our senses take in at any given moment then we wouldn't be able to function at all—that forgetting, and forming a comprehensible narrative from the little we retain, is vital for us to be able to move smoothly though life.

I started to wonder what would happen if, for some reason, someone was to retain every single detail of what they saw at a particular moment. That maybe, although we need to forget most of what we perceive, something is also obscured by that forgetting. That if we could contain it in our heads, even just what is seen in the fraction of a second, something might be unlocked about the mystery and beauty of life. Something that we do sense, but cannot normally access.

And because I wasn't really interested in the actual psychology of it, rather just the idea, I conceived of an entirely fantastical way in which this might happen. That's where the absurdity comes in I suppose. Creating a fantastical plot gives me an arena in which to explore ideas, rather than just situations. But I'm always very interested in interior lives so it's important to me that my characters are real.

The irony of the term Outsider Art—how it uses the language of the establishment to describe an artistic practice that, by definition, exists outside of that establishment—raises interesting ethical questions about the relationship between dealer and artist, the academy and the impulse to create. Do you think there is a literary equivalent?

The further I got with the novel, the more it became about the idea of creativity. I became interested in exploring the creative impulse itself—of how something immaterial becomes translated into something material and the inevitable frustrations and disappointments involved, but also looking at the relationship between the creative impulse and the desire for recognition. I don't think I would write if I didn't have publication as an aim but surely the purest form of creativity is one that doesn't seek recognition. If that is one definition of Outsider Art then I am sure there are literary equivalents. Emily Dickinson is one that springs to mind. She wrote nearly 1,800 poems during her very reclusive life but almost all of these were only discovered after her death.

Literature has no shortage of female muses, who so often function as objects of desire. But Ray's obsession with Jennifer feels very different. How would you describe it?

I didn't want Ray to fall in love with Jennifer or feel desire for her in the conventional sense. I wanted to express the idea that the beauty he sees in her is universal, shared by all humanity, and that he would have seen the same beauty in, and felt the same love for, anybody who happened to have been standing in his field of vision at the time. At the same time, he very specifically sees *her*, which has important consequences for Jennifer. As it says at the end of the book, Ray falls in love, but in love like a fish is in water. His experience immerses him in love itself and provides a direct encounter with another human being, an encounter which is unattainable within normal human relationships.

As interesting—and inscrutable—as Ray is, Jennifer's richly imagined inner life makes her such a compelling character. How do you hope readers are affected by their missed encounter?

It was always very important to me that Ray and Jennifer never actually meet in the novel. I wanted their connection to exist purely in a realm beyond the material world. The ending is a coming together of the characters without them actually coming together. By having them brush past each other without being aware of each other's presence, I wanted to express how the yearning we have for deep connection with the other remains unfulfilled, but only just. We feel the possibility without being able to fully attain it. In many ways the novel is about our inability to truly know each other.